TO: AVA

11-24-2018

A young adult fantasy novel series:
Seal of Excellence from: AwesomeIndies.net

<u>Book One</u> – Deceiver

<u>Book Two</u> – Redeemer

<u>Book Three</u> – Believer

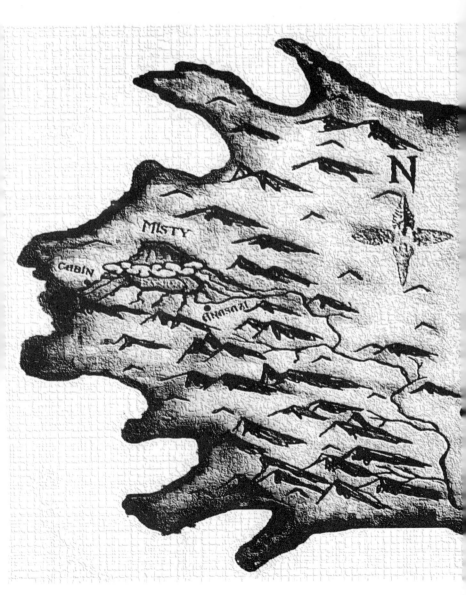

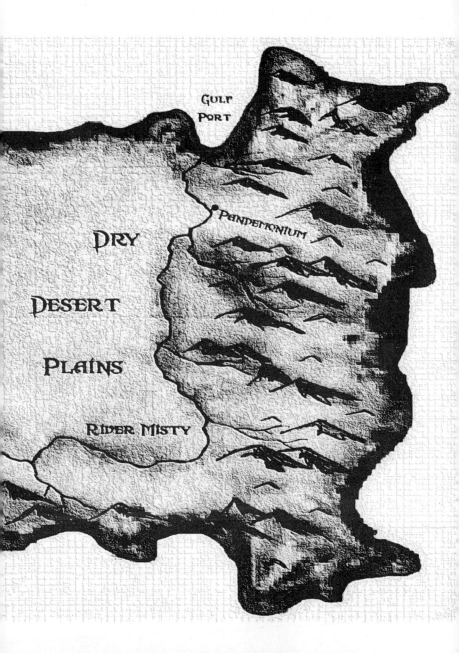

Mystical Mountain Magic
Book 1

Where it all began
Where it all will end...

Dedicated to my girls:
Barbara, Ashley & Tiffiny,
from whom my love and inspiration come.
And to all the dreamers who dare to dream …
may all your dreams, too, come true.

MYSTICAL MOUNTAIN MAGIC

DECEIVER

By:
Guy Brooke

Illustrated by:
Arielle Chandonnet

Mystical Mountain Magic – Deceiver
First in a series of three novels
Text copyright by: Guy Brooke © 2012
Illustrations and graphics © 2013 by: Arielle Marie Chandonnet
◇ ◇ ◇

These books individually or as a set can be purchased in bulk at a discount price for educational, business, fundraising or sales promotional use. For information please contact Mr. Brooke at:
www.GuyBrooke.com
facebook.com/mysticalmountainmagic
◇ ◇ ◇
Library of Congress Registration number: TXu 1-819-796
Conceived, created and published in the USA, by Guy Brooke
◇ ◇ ◇

Summary: Set in early North America, evil fell from the stars and exploded against the mountain. Enticed by this three-legged master musician – the Deceiver – treasure seekers from all over the world come to this unspoiled country in search of their lust's desire. As they create mayhem on this continent, an infant girl – Mariah – is rescued and raised by giant eagles that nest high on the cliffs of Elysium where she is commissioned by the mountain to restore Hope to a world without hope and save mankind from its disastrous effects before the Deceiver can assassinate her.
◇ ◇ ◇

Paperback ISBN# 978-0-9859412-0-8

Table of Contents

The poem that started it all

When I was eighteen I walked along this Colorado mountain lake at night—Twin Lakes. The air was warm, the moon was full, its light shimmered across the still waters. Images flooded my mind as words tried to express the cavalcade of emotions. A story emerged and I have been haunted by its ode ever since. Keeping close to its original draft, it is my sentiment to galvanize this poem in honor of its inspiration.

On the other side of the ode you're about to enter Mystical Mountain Magic's three part novel, crafted for young adult readers in search of exploring a new world of fantasy, allegorical creatures and the ever elusive fountain of youth. So come on in and meet the family—warts and all—there's lots of room!

Guy

Way up on Misty Mountain, where moose migrate to mate
mists of vapor moisture gather at its misty mountain lake
And through these mists, on Misty Mountain
a great white eagle soars
as the twinkle of moonlight magic shimmers lightly by her shore
Now legends mention the moods of this mountain
and where this great white eagle came
And how she may cause her mountain to moan or play music
for Mariah is her name
Mariah, once a young and beautiful maiden, was also very shy
She was loved by all, but the only love she could give
was to that misty mountain sky
She had long dreamed of being Queen
and to rule her secret throne
to either be a part of this mountain or die
for she was to seek its secrets alone
As the next morning whispered its song
Mariah climbed this mountain with a feeling that something was
wrong
She climbed past its high valley in search of an answer
then mists stormed in from nowhere and the mountain began to stir
Up from its marrow the mountain's voice cried
In hot molten tears that have long since dried
Mariah laughed with magic as she sang with the mountain
then she became this white mighty eagle
as she was bathed in the marrow's fountain. . .
Now still today few men will say
that in the distance at the edge of night
Mists will ever guard this mountain
and Mariah's magic coat of white

Prologue

A flash of light splintered the darkness, illuminating the mountain that towered high above the plains. A ring of blood-red fire blasted from its mouth and punched through the earth's atmosphere. For a moment, the stars blew out.

All was black.

The world stood in silence.

Violently ripped from space by the mountain's blast, a creature fell to earth. Multicolored flames trailed the heavenly body as it tore across the sky and exploded against the mountain. The heavens, weeping for their loss, cried sparks in the shooting star's wake—Leira would be missed.

Chapter 1
Elysium

"Wahoo!"

Skye stood on a rock jumping and waving his arms in excitement. He couldn't have known his shouts were about to start a cataclysmic event for the mountain and its inhabitants.

"Wahoo!"

The cool, crisp morning left the young pioneer's skin tingling and his eyes shone as bright as the spring day. Above him, shafts of sunlight pierced the heavy mist that shrouded the towering volcano known as Misty. Down the mountain behind him, his cabin lay at the edge of the forest where a meadow began. Inside, a flame burned in the fireplace and water boiled for tea. Beyond a curtain in their one-room home, his wife, Pearl, and their newborn child lay in bed, asleep beside the warmth of the fire that crackled on the grate.

"This, my love," he said, "is as great a day as ever I've seen. Do wake soon and be glad in it. As for me ..."

He hoisted his musket to his shoulder. "I go where the mountain sings and food waits to be gathered."

With the agility of a deer, he ascended the steep terrain, and his breath came in ragged pulls. He reached the upper ridge of the summit and brushed golden hair from his brow, then froze. For a moment, he couldn't speak. A place he'd once heard of lay sprawled in a valley on the other side of the ridge.

"Elysium," he whispered.

A lush, green valley surrounding a pristine lake opened before him. In random places on the mountainside, he counted seven caves where water shot out and crashed down its rocky face. They flowed together into a single river and spilled over a cliff into the valley. Its roar echoed in the distance.

Above Misty's paradise, eagles—three times the size of normal eagles—glided on the warm breeze. They brushed the wind with golden feathers and tumbled in play at the waterfall's edge.

In the center of the lake, a circle of darker water caught his attention—an indication of greater depths into the heart of the mountain. *A hole*, he thought. *A hole* ...

He remembered a 'hole' in his life and thought back to when he first came to this new world as a stowaway aboard the ship of the Old Norse. While others dreamed of treasure, spices, and finding the fountain of youth, Skye simply wanted to escape the corrupt city of his birth and to climb out of the hole of poverty he'd been buried in. But the captain discovered him aboard ship—the assault still echoed in his mind:

"Drag the rat-boy here, men, an' tie his thievin' hands high." The captain had barked the order. "You there!" He'd jabbed a finger like a knife. "Fetch me whip, now!"

They'd thrust him against the mast, and the splinters

pricked at him. Then he'd seen the ghostly bloodstains from past tortures—his blood soon joined them.

The floggings had been brutal, and the toils as a slave still made his insides tie up in knots. He rotated his shoulders, feeling the damage. Even after all this time, his body had not healed fully, and he feared the mental scars would take longer.

If not for the favor found in the eyes of the captain's daughter, Pearl, he would have drowned in a sea of hopelessness. Pearl, too, knew well the depth of her father's cruelty, and carried the marks to prove it. A shiver crawled up Skye's spine as he recalled the patchwork of welts left on her body and he fought to hold back his anger.

He focused his attention back to the present, and a weight lifted from him. The vast view of Elysium evoked a sense of freedom that made him want to shout and dance. But something happened right then that transfixed him—a voice singing in the woods.

He cocked his head to one side and listened. Its melody—light and airy—sailed like a sparrow in play, and he became lost in its tantalizing eddy.

Chimes, like water rippling down a stream, echoed from hollow, golden strands of hair. Something evil stalked the nearby woods; it prowled closer to its victim, singing its hypnotic song.

The creature, invisible to this world, tried to materialize but couldn't fully form. Like a floating jigsaw puzzle, portions of its body appeared, then disappeared and reappeared again. Off and on, in and out, the creature flashed in pieces. Puffs of sulfuric smoke blew from its nostrils, up from its chest where a crusted heart thumped to the rhythm of its song. Its mission was vindictive, and its anger set on the one who tore it from the heavens. To avenge, it needed to be physical.

In a silver robe, it roamed the shadows of the woods, following Skye's joyous shouts. Silver lips sang over lethal teeth. Jeweled fingernails flexed and snagged a pine tree as it walked past, dislodging bark and raking deep lines into the wood—it hated jubilation, loathed its spirit! Music and mirth had been the creature's profession, but now it needed to destroy everything joyous, righteous or good. Slowly—in and out, on and off—the creature crept toward its prey.

A squirrel chattered, waking Skye from the song's hypnosis.

The music stopped.

Skye shook his head and tried to gather his thoughts. Emptiness replaced the music. An aching need, greater than hunger, pulled at his soul. He wanted more. Much more.

Something tickled at his face. He brushed a knuckle up his cheek and looked at it—a tear. Never had he been so deeply touched. He looked around but couldn't find the songstress.

The mysterious music and the discovery of Elysium overwhelmed him—he had to tell someone. Down the mountain he could see his cabin, partially hidden by the edge of the woods. Pearl, awake now, hung the wash on a rope stretched between two trees. Their newborn lay swaddled in the grass beside her.

"Pearl!" Skye shouted and waved for the sheer joy of it. She'd never be able to hear from that distance, but he didn't care. "Hey, Pearl. *Wahoo!*" Then he danced through the scattered trees like a wild gypsy.

Skye's voice echoed across the landscape. In response, the earth trembled beneath his feet and rocks tumbled from above.

Deep inside the mountain, molten rock roiled. On the lava's surface, an enormous eye opened and blinked. Within the reflection of the eye, an image danced—a newcomer to the area, yet already known by the mountain. With ancient patience, it observed Skye.

"It is time for this young seed to grow, my friend," the voice of the mountain bubbled.

"True, it is," replied a gravelly voice. "But remember, before a flower can grow, the seed must first die."

"Yes, it must," replied the mountain. "So now it begins?"

"From the beginning of creation we knew this would come. Yes, finally, it is time."

Chapter 2
Clouds in the Skye

Misty shook. Skye cast a frightened gaze around and staggered but managed to retain his footing. The earth cracked beneath him and clouds billowed like an avalanche from the top of the mountain. Shockwaves of fear shot through his body.

An ash storm thundered towards him, about to hit. Behind, an angelic song raked his soul like sugarcoated fingernails across his heart—sweet yet dangerous. With no time to shield himself against the impending storm, he whirled to see what voice sang to his soul, but it was too late. A blast of wind knocked him to the ground, snapping his hair and clothes like whips.

He closed his eyes against the swirling ash, and wild wind-blown moments passed. Then a hush melted over the mountainside. Save for the heaving of his chest and the rapid beat of his heart, all became still. The angelic voice had vanished along with Skye's musket.

He wiped the grit from his face and shook it from his hair. Somewhere in the fog and settling ash, the mysterious voice wailed, and the dissonant notes shivered over his skin. His dream world had turned into a living nightmare.

"What on Earth?" He waved a ghostly hand in front of his eyes, but couldn't see a thing.

Cold fingers of fear reached into his mind, and his chest tightened. He groped for something solid to hold onto but found nothing except the earth beneath his hands and knees.

"Steady now, Skye." He tried to calm himself. "You've been in bad situations before, so think—it's fear touching you, not some bear. If you can beat fear, then you've won."

He stood. The earth trembled again, but he rode it like a bucking horse.

"You hear that, fear?" he shouted. "I know who you are, and I fear … you … not!"

On that word, Misty stood still as death.

"See? See?" the gravelly voice said. "I told you this could be the one foreseen. Remember? It was written long ago:

> *"Ever since the days of yore,*
> *Men would fight, men would war,*
> *It spread like fire, it blew like wind.*
> *Grass was greener in this distant land*
> *But attitudes wailed, and failed morals grew*
> *Like a rock's ripple spreading in a pool*
> *They heard of something nice, it seemed*
> *But they had to take it and make it unclean*
> *'To the mountain!' they cried in rage.*
> *'Take their treasure! Lock the cage!'*
> *The only village left to die*

> *Would soon be safe under Misty's sky*
> *Reverse the shame. Turn back time.*
> *A seed must come to break the line*
> *A rock he found. A rock he threw,*
> *To start a ripple fresh and new."*

"Yes, I think you're right," the mountain said in a gurgle. "But are you sure the prophecy translates to 'he'?"

"It is an uncertain interpretation, no doubt," the gravelly voice muttered, "but all signs do lead to this young man, I'm sure—I think."

"You think? Well, we'll soon see. When ready, you may lead him on, my friend, lead him on."

A transparent dome rose from the ground beneath Skye and expanded upward, like a bubble blown by a giant. He jumped back, but the bubble-dome moved with him and billowed up his legs and to his waist. He tried to step out of it, but it stretched with his movement. He tried pushing it away, but it kept growing around him.

"What's happening? What is this?" His words lumped in his throat, and anxiety swelled with the bubble when it crept past his chest and up his outstretched neck. Once it reached his chin, he took a deep breath and the liquid dome pushed up and over his head, sealing him inside. When his lungs were about to burst, he exhaled with reluctance and breathed in. A flood of foreign gas filled his lungs.

Poison!

Certain of his fate, he rushed towards the membrane, hoping to rip it apart. But as he moved forward, so did the bubble, wobbling just out of reach. When he realized that he wasn't dying, he relaxed and breathed easier. The gas smelled of spice—something like Aspen trees and cinnamon. A few more breaths and his mind cleared. Relief washed over him, and strength returned to his limbs.

He surveyed the situation from inside the six-foot dome that entrapped him. Outside, the fog swirled, trying—it seemed—to get in, as if it wanted to touch him.

He stepped forward, and the bubble moved forward. He stopped, and the bubble stopped. When he walked, the bubble kept up with him. He tried to outrun it, but the flexible dome always moved along the ground with him, keeping him encased.

At first, Skye found roaming in his protective dome fascinating, but when he tried to turn toward home, the bubble pushed him back the other way. He tripped over rocks, stumbling on unpredictable ground. In frustration, he lashed out at the wobbly skin. His fist hit the wall but the membrane stretched under the force and sprang back.

He glared at his cage. "I will not be held against my will—not again. Let me out, I need to go home."

As if in answer, the dome slid forward and nudged him. Skye stumbled a few steps. The dome nudged him again. "No!" He pushed it back. "I will not be a sheep led to slaughter!"

In angry protest he sat down and crossed his arms. The earth rumbled and the eerie snapping of granite beneath him escalated. The dome nudged again, but Skye remained unmoved. The dome waited a minute then moved. This time it purposely passed over Skye and left him sitting unprotected in the cold.

"Hey." Skye jumped to his feet. Ice crystals formed

over his clothes and skin and his chest tightened with fear. Frantic, he searched around for shelter, but could only see a circle of visible ground a few feet away—his prison waited to receive him back.

He ran to the dome and shuffled around the perimeter, slapped at its surface and looked for a way back in, but found none. "Let me in, *please*, I'm freezing."

The bubble did not respond, and left Skye in the harsh elements. Desperate to get back in, he flattened his hand and thrust it like a knife into the bubble's side. It slipped through the wall of the bubble. He slid his other hand in beside it and, with a bit of effort, widened the gap. He pushed his shoulder into the wedge, forcing his upper torso through. From the waist he dangled in midair, pushing against the inner wall until he flopped back into the safety of the dome, exhausted and shivering.

The dome nudged him. "All right, I'm coming, I'm coming; just don't leave me like that again," he said, while rubbing warmth back into his arms. "Whatever you are, lead me on. Let's get this over with."

The bubble nudged him along on a determined path, turning only to avoid boulders or trees. Sometimes their passage dislodged rocks and sent them tumbling off the side of the mountain into the abyss.

The farther he drifted, the more anxious he became. Leery to leave his elastic room, he thought it wise to tread carefully and see where it led him. Steadily, he marched, not knowing where or why, only that he must.

Morning turned to noon and noon to evening. Exhaustion settled over Skye, and his belly grumbled for a meal much the same way as the ground grumbled under his feet. Just when he thought he would wander the mountain forever, the bubble stopped.

Slowly, the dome melted back into the earth, leaving

him exposed to the elements again. Cold fingers of fog prickled his skin.

The mountain shook harder, and dislodged stones showered like hail, bumping and crashing around him. In a slide of pelting debris, a large rock bowled Skye over the embankment. Pain seized his body as he hit the slope, and he tumbled faster and faster in the slide until he hurtled through the air and off a jagged cliff. Thoughts of Pearl and their baby went through his mind, and his heart faltered.

Together, they'd fought for their freedom. They'd been hunted; they'd run; they'd hidden and struggled in the wilderness. Eventually, they'd eluded their predators and found peace on the mountain. Skye had a well-earned life, but now—just like that—gone. It wasn't fair!

"Noooo!" he screamed through the air, and then his foggy world went black.

"Good shot. Couldn't have done it better myself," said the gravelly voice. "Your aim's getting better all the time."

The mountain groaned.

"Hey, don't be so hard on yourself."

"Well, don't you think we've been a little hard on him?" the mountain gurgled back.

"Ah, nonsense." He chuckled and gave a wave of his hand. "He'll bounce right back, you'll see. Good as new, guaranteed."

"We really should see how—"

"He's strong, you know. Vigorous, you might say. Hmm, I wonder how he's doing? Really now, you ought to be a little more careful in these situations."

Once the mountain's companion got started it was hard to stop him, so he interjected quickly, "Nothing must happen to the man. We really must—"

"But, on the other hand," the gravelly voice said as he made his way down a tunnel, "I must hurry to help the poor fellow, so we'll have to visit later. I know it's a little rude to leave so abruptly like this, but duty calls. I'd best be on my way at once. However, it will take some time to get there from here. If you mark the distance, it might take a while. Now, why wasn't I there already to greet him properly? It isn't like you to forget things like that, you know. I mean, how often do we have such honored guests? In the future, we must be more ..."

The gravelly voice rambled on about proper protocols of politeness, the past, the present, and the things foretold to come as he made his way down the crystal-lit caverns.

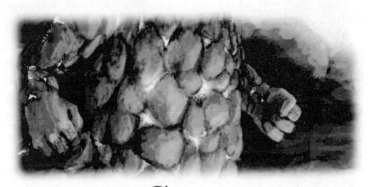

Chapter 3

Igneous

Skye stirred and opened his eyes just as the sun touched the horizon. Waves of pain shot through his body making spots appear before his eyes. He found himself sprawled on a narrow parapet and if he could have seen beyond the fog to the jagged rocks below, the little blood left in his veins would have curdled.

He touched his brow, and his fingers came away smeared with blood. His leg throbbed—a bone protruded from his flesh over a puddle of blood. He struggled to sit up, but it made him dizzy. He squeezed his eyes shut and eased back down. He was alive that's all he knew.

A warm breeze ruffled his hair and caressed his cold flesh. The scent of spice, wholesome and rich like in the bubble, floated in its current. The fragrance cleared his mind and he lifted his head. The breeze parted the fog around him enough to reveal a four-foot archway into the mountain, crafted in marble and polished to a gleaming white. Ancient etchings and script intertwined around images of the animals, people, and eagles under Misty's domain covered every inch of the arch. Beyond the archway, red lights pulsed.

Goosebumps nettled his arms. *I'm freezing. I've got to get inside.* He dug his fingers into the cracks of the parapet and, leaving a trail of blood behind, scooted his broken body close enough to grab the archway and drag himself inside. He lay exhausted within the warmth of the cave and wondered at the red glow around him.

Am I dreaming, or have I just entered a cave of demons? Deeemons ... He fell in the dirt and lost consciousness.

Poke—poke

Skye jerked awake with his mouth half pushed into the dusty floor. One bloodshot eye fluttered open. A few feet from his head, sat a large boulder the size of a man. He spat dirt from his mouth and felt the boulder's heat on his face.

Poke—poke

Something jabbed at him again.

Slowly, painfully, he leaned his body to one side to get a clearer look. A series of lines cracked open on the surface of the boulder. They branched out in different directions, popping and snapping as they went. A teal light swelled through the cracks, and the boulder hummed as if it breathed. Two crystal eyes popped open on the top, and a stony mouth splintered open below them.

Skye's eyes rolled back inside his head.

Poke—poke—poke. A stony finger jabbed insistently. "Wahoo," it whispered, as Skye faded away. "Wahoo," it cried louder in imitation of Skye's shouts earlier that morning.

Skye flinched. "Aaagh!" With the heel of his good foot, he pushed himself against the cave wall, waving a hand in warning. "Get away from me. Get away!"

The boulder ignored the plea and rolled closer. "You disturbed our rest." Its voice sounded like rocks tumbling in a wooden drum. "Nevertheless, welcome stranger."

An arm grew from its side. "Well, maybe not so much a stranger, because we've known about you for quite some time now." Another arm grew from the opposite side. "Perhaps a millennia or two, I guess." It scratched its temple with a stony finger.

Skye fainted.

Thud! Dust flew up from the floor and the young man's face pushed into the dirt—again.

"Hmm." The rock creature rolled closer and studied the situation. Shingled lids blinked over its crystal eyes. "Oh my, I had no idea." The earthen creature pushed a thick, stony hand under Skye's shoulder and lifted him to one side. "Hmm, now," it said, then put him back down and rolled to the other side of the young man. Puzzled, it leaned over and slid its finger across the floor. "Would you look at all the dust blown in. Doesn't go well with the floor design at all, not at all. Knew I should have made a door."

After fussing a bit more about the unkempt room, the boulder looked again on its guest then spoke to the ceiling. "Perhaps you overdid it this time, you suppose?"

The mountain rumbled in response.

"Honestly," the creature replied with a shrug, "I thought the man was strong. Oh well, can't blame him, you know; he does seem a little beat up and all. Not at all rock-like. Hmmm."

It leaned closer to check Skye's physical condition.

"No matter, we'll fix him up in no time. He'll be good as new, you'll see."

The glowing boulder placed an object in front of Skye, then sat patiently and stared down at his guest.

At length, Skye stirred, once more spitting dirt from his mouth.

"Hello, again, my fragile friend," the boulder said. "Didn't mean to scare you, you know? It's been so long since we allowed guests to come to our home, and I guess we got a little excited. You understand, don't you?"

Skye opened one eye. A rock the size of a cantaloupe sat inches from his face, blocking the view of the boulder behind it. It, too, pulsed a teal light from the cracks in its surface.

"Here, let me help you," the rock host said. Arms of stone lifted Skye to a sitting position against the wall.

Hundreds of glowing stones bordered the grotto, and they all pulsed and emitted a soft purr. It sounded as if the room were full of sleeping kittens.

Certainly no ordinary cave of earth and bugs, as he'd first thought, but a cave in which cut rubies polished to a gleam studded every inch of the walls. A matrix of gold welded each ruby into place, forming a dome-shaped grotto large enough to hold a few dozen men.

Refracted light, fed by the glowing stones, sparkled throughout the room like a million red stars. So spectacular the sight, a person could become spellbound by the flawless beauty—a stunning trap for intruders.

On the opposite side of the grotto, three arched corridors tunneled deep into the heart of the mountain, each lined with the same glowing stones.

"There, now." The boulder patted Skye's shoulder, and sent dust flying with each pat. "Hmm, you sure took some nasty spills, didn't you?" It crossed its rocky arms. "But not to worry, oh no, you'll be good as new, you'll see. Then there's something we'd like you to do for us."

"Am I your prisoner?" Skye asked, rubbing a hand across his face. Dust fell from his hair.

"Oh no, you mustn't think—"

"Then I'm your slave."

"Slave!?"

"Ah, you admit it."

"No, no, not at all, you—"

"I was once a slave, Mr. Rock, or whatever kind of creature you are, and I swore I'd never be one again."

"Now there's no need to—"

"Your greed is great, Mr. Rock," Skye said, while he analyzed the room. "And you seem to have quite a taste for riches. Where is my shovel, creature, so I may dig more gold and gems for your crypt?" He struggled to get up, but his crippled leg hurt too much. "Unless you prefer to watch me use my hands."

"Not slave. Not prisoner. You must relax." It placed its hand on Skye's shoulder and lowered him back down with a gentle touch.

Skye slouched, against the wall, exhausted. Beads of sweat speckled his face. "Then why was I brought here against my will?"

"Good question, indeed. There is a good reason for everything we do, but you must be patient. We do things a little different around here, as you'll soon see."

The rock-creature reached down and lifted the throbbing stone. "It is for you to know firsthand the power of these oracles."

With one swift thrust, it cracked the stone open against its side and the stone glowed no more.

"Here, have some. It tickles a bit going down, but it's guaranteed to make you feel better." The boulder pulled the stone apart like a coconut and held it out to him. "Come now, no time to be shy, I always say. Drink."

Skye eyed the creature while picking more dirt from his lips, then he lifted his head enough to peek inside the stone's shell. His eyes widened at the sight of the thick, teal liquid swirling about inside. Cautious, he took one of the half-shells, gazed into its contents, and breathed in its fragrance.

"Please," the creature said, "drink, it will make you well, you'll see."

Skye pushed two fingers into the warm liquid, lifted them out, and it absorbed into his skin, smooth as oil. He flinched at the sensation. With every beat of Skye's heart, the stone's blood tingled up his fingers and through his arm. It invigorated and strengthened him, but his leg still hurt. His broken shin bone pierced the skin at an unnatural angle, and pushed through his torn pants.

The earthen creature smiled. "If you don't feel like drinking yet, my skeptical friend, then let the stone's blood anoint every wound and bruise. Like this." He tipped his shell and a small stream of liquid flowed over the protruding bone.

Skye flinched again, but relaxed when the fluid soothed his pain. Then something tugged at his bone. It pulled, squeezed, and tightened until the bone snapped back into place. The pain disappeared. He examined his leg: no wound, no blood, not even a scar.

A surge of energy suddenly shot through him and he jumped to his feet. He rammed his head into the curve of the ruby-studded wall and crumbled back to the cobbled ground.

The creature shook his head. "Remedy-rush. Be careful of the remedy-rush."

Skye rubbed his forehead with one hand and held out the other. "Pass the stone, please," he whispered.

The creature scooted one of the shells to Skye and continued as if nothing had happened. "You see, my hyper fellow, these stones are not ordinary by any means. They are living-stones, brewed back when the earth was fresh and new."

It held up another stone and inspected it, turning it back and forth on the tips of rocky fingers. "These stones possess the very lifeblood of this planet." Its voice rolled with passion as it observed the oracle. "It packs quite a punch, wouldn't you agree?"

Skye tried to speak, but the stone's glow and purring voice held him transfixed. Not until the creature hid the stone behind its back was Skye released from its hold. "Who are you?" he asked, blinking moisture back into his eyes.

"Oh, my, yes, where are my manners?" The creature straightened. "My name is Igneous, the gardener and guardian of these caverns and all that is within them. Pleased to make your acquaintance. I'm at your service, master Skye." He bowed.

"Now ..." He pointed his thick finger. "If you dip back into the stone's blood and place it on the knock your head just received, I'm sure you'll find it most satisfying. Go on."

Skye reached into the shell, drizzled the syrup on his head, then leaned back with a sigh—the pain shriveled away. He put his lips to the edge of the stony grail and sipped its contents as if it were hot soup on a cold day. The stone's life coursed through his veins and his taste buds came alive. A remedy-rush hit him again.

He sat straight up and talked fast. "Where am I? I was trapped inside a bubble and it brought me here. Do you know anything about bubbles? The mountain shook and—wham—rocks swept me over a cliff. I thought I was dead. And there you were, poking me, and you wouldn't stop poking. Poke—poke—poke, over and over again. Are you responsible for all this? What kind of creature are you, anyway?"

"Whoa, now." Igneous held up a stony hand. "No more sips for you. First things first, if you please." He took the shell from Skye.

"Responsible for bringing you here, you ask? Well, yes. It was my idea for the bubble, of course. I wanted to make sure you were led safely along the rugged terrain without getting hurt."

Skye rolled his eyes. "Good job. Very thoughtful of you. Well done, I must say. Didn't hurt at all. Eh-eh, not—a—bit."

"It was Misty's idea to shake you off the mountainside, not mine. Well … okay, I had a little to do with it, too. It was the one way to get you to the only entrance here, except the big one on top. But, I assure you, that way is detrimental to a mortal's existence. I designed it myself—designed everything you see here, inside and out. It took a long time too, I might add, but it was worth every century of it—seven thousand seven-hundred and seventy-seven to be exact. And I gained a lifelong friend out of it as well, although I don't quite know how long 'lifelong' really is for Misty and me. I suppose we'll find out someday. However, for you and mankind in general, lifelong is quite short, quite fragile, and, unfortunately, quite corrupt. I've been around to see it all, you know. That's why you're here now—to help put back in time what was lost through the ages."

"Lost?" Skye stood carefully, so as not to knock his head again on the curved wall, and walked around to get the feeling back in his leg and work out some kinks. "You mean like the rubies on your walls and other treasures?"

"Oh, no, my ambitious explorer." Igneous wagged his finger while following his pacing guest. "Jewels and any other worldly things that rust or rot or get eaten by something have very little value with us. It was Hope. For without Hope, why try to do what's right, hmm? It's always easier for a corrupt man to fall back to his natural ways of corruptness than for him to believe and hold fast to something better—that which is good and honest. There would be no patience. Why hope for tomorrow's fortune if it can be forced or stolen today?"

"I see. Why would Pearl and I plant crops in spring if we didn't have hope for a harvest in autumn?"

"Ah, now you see. Without hope, human morality has a hard time staying together. It's sort of like ethical glue that goes beyond ... are you all right?"

Skye looked away in troubled thought.

"Hmm, it's Pearl, isn't it? I saw it in your eyes the moment you spoke of planting crops with her. You're wondering if you'll ever see your family again, aren't you?"

"It has crossed my mind." Skye kicked some dirt around on the floor. "But I seem to be losing hope."

"Hope, there it goes again. Now don't you be fretting. I assure you, the two of you will be together again. But first, we're hoping you'll help with this 'Hope' dilemma of ours. After that, have quality time with your loved ones, my friend, for they are a treasure all too easily lost, and your time with them may just about be up."

"Excuse me?"

Igneous froze. "Oops, can't say any more than I've already said, and perhaps I shouldn't have even said that.

Oh well, what's done is done." He reached over and ruffled Skye's hair. "We like you, Skye, and we want you to make the best of life before it, too, is gone. Live this day well or it may disappear before you know it, like fog."

Skye brushed the hair back out of his eyes and leaned forward. "Igneous, you're starting to scare me. If I understand you correctly, and my days are limited, then what hope do I have?"

"Ah, I see what you mean. You're feeling the effects of hopelessness, aren't you? So is the rest of the world. You wouldn't be saying that if Hope was back in the world, would you?"

"I don't know—it's hard to think right now."

"Let me help you, if I can. This hopeless dilemma is being experienced by everyone, man and beast. But it can be solved, I assure you. We have a plan, master Skye, but your help is required ... if you're willing."

Skye leaned his back against the curved wall, and tried to sort out his feelings. He looked around the ruby room then back into the crystal eyes of his host. "I don't like what's happening to me and the world, Igneous. It makes me feel ... less than a man. I want to help, but I also need to return to my home. What should I do?"

For a moment, the guardian considered the question. When he spoke, he chose his words carefully, and leaned over and whispered some instructions into Skye's ear.

Skye lifted an eyebrow and stepped back. "You've got to be jesting."

"Afraid not, my young friend."

"Everything off?"

"Well, most everything, that's for certain. It'll be worth it. Think of it this way: you were chosen thousands of years ago to get these wheels back in motion, so it's bound to work—I hope. No pun intended. But not to worry—you and the living-stone have consumed each other; you are now one. The stone's life will give you strength when you need it and counsel when all words are lost. Make no mistake about it, you have been chosen, master Skye."

"All right." Skye shrugged. "I'll try."

Igneous scrunched his face. "That wasn't very convincing. Is that all you've got?"

Skye straightened his shoulders. "Yes, I'm willing to give it a shot."

"No, no, no, no. Are you in ... or are you out?"

Skye's brows pulled together. "I'm in." he said, a little irritated.

"I caaan't heaaar yooou."

"I *said* ..." Skye walked boldly to the boulder and stared into his crystal eyes. "YES—I get it, life is meaningless without hope and we're all going to give up and die, and for some reason I have a part to play in this restoration. So before I lose all hope and patience, let's get on with it—*now!"*

Igneous declared to the ceiling, "I told you so!"

The mountain rumbled in response.

"I knew it. Grand choice, master Skye, grand choice." he said, patting his shoulder. "Come now, quick, look into the stone. See, you're needed even as we speak." Igneous held out the stone's other half to Skye, rattled his shingled eyelids closed, and raised his head in concentration.

Skye took a few calming breaths before he peeked inside. The syrupy teal elixir swirled into an image. A puzzled look crossed his face.

"Uh, Igneous? Sorry to bother you. I know you're concentrating, but all I see is a reflection of my eye."

"What?" Igneous looked inside the bowl. "Oh, no, that's not your eye, it's Misty." He cleared his throat. "Ho there, thither mountain, cease thy intrusive gaze, wilts' thee?" He looked to Skye. "He just *loves* it when I speak Shakespearian. He also wants to know everything—you know—the all-seeing eye?" He waved his hand then looked back into the stone. "Ah, here we go. Quick, look."

Together with the guardian, Skye gazed into the shell. Images formed in the churning liquid. A vision of the mountain materialized, as if he were looking down over Misty. Scenery drifted by. First, he saw the eastern slope, and then the vision flew down the mountainside, as if riding on the back of an eagle.

The image picked up speed as it descended and raced toward a village at the edge of Misty's timberline. A river flowed around the stick-and-mud thatched homes and out to the valley below. Far away near the horizon, it spilled into a vast body of water where ships and large sea-creatures wandered.

The tops of trees rushed by as the image drew closer to the village. The trees eventually gave way to huts—the people around them busy with daily activities. The image circled the village, looping as it approached the ground and descended in front of the largest hut. A few people walked in with bowls of water, food, and an assortment of ceremonial instruments.

The image in the stone followed one of the women as she pulled a heavy blanket aside, dipped her head, and passed into the hut. The image rose, looking down from the ceiling, allowing Skye to see everything.

In the middle of the hut a small fire burned, its smoke funneling out through a hole in the roof. Beside the fire, a man stood dressed in ceremonial feathers. Red and white paint striped his face. The woman fastened beads and bells around his waist and ankles, and then watched as he danced around the small fire, shaking a club in one hand, and skipping and spinning on the dusty floor.

In the corner, an elderly pregnant woman attended an old man lying still as death on a bed of animal skins. Wounds laced the man's arm, neck, and chest, as if slashed by some wild beast. The strangest wound circled around his heart in a pattern of five festering holes.

The man tossed and turned while the woman washed his wounds.

The painted man's dance became more violent. He chanted, he sang, and he spun and jumped. He smeared red paint across the wounded man's face and chest and shook his club repeatedly, making large gestures with his hands.

Slowly, the image in the shell drifted up and out of the hut with the smoke. It soared into the blue sky and faded back into the color of the stone's swirling elixir, cupped by strong, stony fingers.

Chapter 4
Show and Tell

"Come, walk with me. A grand tour is in order and we can talk as we go." Igneous swooped an arm low through the air, and pointed the way.

The two passed into the center of the three corridors at the back of the cave and wound their way through the mountain. The details of Igneous' workmanship amazed Skye. Everywhere he looked, colored crystals sprang from the walls like flowers along a stream. Even the cobbled floors displayed polished gems that sparkled under his every step.

Igneous spoke to him about his upcoming quest. He spoke also of the mountain's history and about the first people who came to reside in its woods. Skye learned of the giant eagles and a few secrets about the lake.

"It's all in the brew, my dear man, all in the brew. Pure food," Igneous said. "A gift from Misty. You are what you eat, you know. The waters they drink are rich in nutrients that leak out from the living-stones, and the fish that swim in the lake are food that makes the eagles smart. Remarkable, intelligent creatures, they are. Makes them grow large, too. And—even though we really don't need the help—they like to guard our mountain. That's dedication any father would be proud of."

Sky noticed many times that they crossed intersecting tunnels and entered other domed caverns. Each cavern was the same shape and size as the others but featured a different gem studding the walls. They passed through rooms of diamond, topaz, beryl, onyx, jasper, turquoise, emerald, and many others—all polished and welded in place with gold. The sight took his breath away each time they entered a room. It also took some willpower, and at times a nudge from Igneous, to step out of those rooms.

Igneous had purposely designed the mountain this way to hold captive any trespassers. The whole system was a maze—a spider's web of complexity.

"Why all the security?" Skye asked. "It's difficult enough to find the entrance, let alone the way out."

"Quite right, my curious friend." Igneous stopped and faced Skye, leaned forward, and became deadly serious. "But someone has, or should I say," his eyes shifted left then right, "some 'thing'."

"Thing?" Skye didn't like the sound of that.

"It's the best description that fits."

"How so?"

The guardian crossed his arms, eyes squinted in thought. "Only once through the ages has someone broken in. At night, a thief came. Fragments of living-stones lay scattered, their blood smeared everywhere. Murdered." His voice shook. "I heard my stones through the corridors—hundreds of them screaming as they died. No reason for the murders other than for the pleasure of hearing my oracles cry. The murderer slipped away as easily as he came before I could get to him."

"Did you get a look at whatever it was?"

"No. At first we believed we knew who it might be,

but what we found puzzled us. Whatever it was ..." The guardian's eyes flashed and narrowed, sending shivers over Skye's arms. "It walks on ... three legs ... six toes each. The strangest thing I've ever seen, and it made sure I'd see its tracks in the blood on my floors." He looked straight into Skye's frightened eyes and whispered, "We have been visited—again."

Igneous' rocky muscles flexed before the boulder relaxed with a sigh.

"Last night it tried to come in through one of the seven water-light towers."

"Why did it come back?"

Rocky shoulders shrugged. "Sometimes people get used to the shameful things they do. They do what is wrong for so long that it becomes natural. They reason what's bad to be good, and they continue wallowing in it—even start to enjoy it. Stolen fruit is sweet, my friend, but soon grows sour. That's when immorality takes its toll."

The guardian looked around with eyes narrowed. "So if you see anything unusual you will let me know, won't you?"

"Anything unusual?" Skye chuckled. "Everything here is unusual. How am I to know?"

"Hmm, good point, my befuddled fellow, but I can reassure you ..." He put a hand to Skye's shoulder. "... you'll know it in your heart—if you can trust what is there. Trusting is a hard thing to do, I know, but you must learn to do it, particularly in situations you don't fully understand. You'll see what I mean about trust soon enough."

He ruffled Skye's hair again. "Come now, our tour is almost at an end."

Skye wasn't sure he liked the way Igneous talked

about trusting. He brushed his mussed hair back out of his eyes and chewed his lower lip.

They entered another grotto—one made of sapphires. This one resembled the others, except it held a larger stone, shaped like a teardrop. About half the size of Igneous, the stone rested in the center of the room like a trophy. It hummed in deeper tones than the smaller living-stones, but not as deeply as Igneous himself.

Igneous stopped at the oracle, ran his hand over its surface, and spoke encouragingly. "All in good time, my child, and you shall be free once more. Chains will be broken again because of you, you'll see. But first things first."

The teardrop stone purred louder in Igneous' presence. He made no explanation to Skye, and continued his tour through the room as if nothing had happened.

Skye eyed the large stone as he walked past. "What was that about?" Igneous swiveled around, looking puzzled, then lifted his gravelly brows. "What? Oh—why, yes, where are my manners?"

He rolled back to Skye, took hold of his hand, and placed it on top of the oracle.

"Master Skye, you are with Hope."

Silver sparks flickered off the surface under Skye's hand and showered to the ground. Hope jerked and glowed brighter.

Skye's legs gave out and he collapsed to his knees, unable to remove his hand from Hope. Tears sprang to his eyes. Hope had a purpose—its urgency real. Skye's mouth hung open and the oracle's words spilled from him, resounding deep and earthy in the chamber.

> *"I cry. I weep. I mourn in pain*
> *My children, are you well?*
> *Are you valiant? Are you sane?*
> *I worry how you rest, if you run while troubles chase*
> *I long to encourage you, to show you there is grace*
> *To hold you, to mold you in my arms safe and tight*
> *To wake you, to shake you, to whisper 'It's all right'*
> *I cry. I weep. I mourn in pain*
> *My children, are you well?*
> *Are you valiant? Are you sane?"*

As quickly as they began, the sparks stopped. A cold wave of goosebumps hit him. "She ... she spoke through me," he finally gasped out.

"Yes, my boy." Igneous bent over and put a comforting hand on his back. "Hope sings her song to me over and over again, in much the same way. But the feelings go deeper, don't they?"

Skye sat with his back against Hope, and wiped the moisture from his eyes with the heel of his hand. "She aches, Igneous. Aches to be back in the world, back with her children—us—mankind."

For once Igneous seemed at a loss for words. With a nod he let Skye know that he understood.

"Igneous?"

"Yes?"

"Why is Hope in this room and not out where she wants to be? How did she even get here?"

"All good questions, my friend, but not easy to answer, I'm afraid." He crossed one arm in front of himself and placed his other elbow on top. With his finger and thumb, Igneous pinched his stony lip in thought. "Hmm, perhaps I should start by first saying ... Misty is very sick."

"Misty's sick?" Skye sat up.

"Yes, well; maybe, I should say, depressed."

"Depressed?"

"Yep! Well, perhaps it's more like he's really worried."

"Worried?"

"Well, of course. Wouldn't you be sick, depressed, and worried if you just learned that Hope is dying?"

"Hope is dying?"

"Is there an echo in here? Hmm, I thought I insulated better than that." Igneous went to the wall and patted it, feeling its integrity.

"Igneous, is this all true?"

"Yes. Unfortunately, it is so." The light in Igneous' eyes dimmed. "Like a rock's ripple in a pool, man has steadily become more degenerate, greedy, and violent. Kindness for kindness's sake has become the exception to the rule. Wealth, instead of good deeds, now measures success. Because of this, I saw Misty cry. Never thought he could do it, but there it was—a tear. It wept right out of the lake down below and left a deep, dark hole in the center."

Skye remembered seeing the dark spot in the lake earlier that day.

"This teardrop is made up of all that is precious to life. It is, in all actuality, the heart of Misty. From that day, Hope began to die. The only hope for her survival is the same hope for man's survival: to put back into time— once and for all—Hope.

"Hope has been draining slowly from the world for quite some time now. How long Hope's residue on the world will last is unknown, but it can't be much longer. It is said that there is always hope, however ..." He paused, face solemn. "I seriously wonder if there will be any left for mankind."

"Can't you put it back?"

"I can't do it, Skye. It would mean nothing if it came from me. I'm not the one chosen for this calling. Hope must be dropped back into Elysium Lake, and she must penetrate the very hole from which she came—the heart of Misty. Only the chosen one will be able to accomplish it."

"How will you know who is chosen?"

"By their devotion to Misty. It will be the one who has fallen unconditionally in love with the mountain and all he stands for—the one who's willing to be changed for the sake of putting Hope back into the world. Then and only then will Hope live and be restored for all."

"And you believe I'm that chosen one, don't you? Otherwise, why would you bring me here?"

"What does your heart tell you?"

"My heart?" Skye reflected for a moment. "My heart is confused. I've been gone too long and too much has happened to me to think with my head, much less my heart." He leaned against Hope, and looked away in thought. "I do know I love my family and what I've come to see as my home, and I'm devoted to all that surrounds me. That is one thing my heart and I are clear on."

"And that is a very good place to start." Igneous nodded. "So, be of good cheer. Whether or not you are the chosen one, you are fulfilling your part accordingly."

Skye stared. "The man we saw in the stone, he's hurt bad, isn't he?"

"Oh yes, absolutely—right at death's door even as we speak. You know, if we don't get you there as soon as possible, the Chief will die." Igneous nudged Skye with his elbow. "Hey, want to see where the water comes gushing out of the mountain into the waterfall? The best view you'll ever see is right around this corner."

Skye stood. "Hold on, you just can't switch subjects like that. You're telling me that was a chief we saw?"

"Why yes. Chief Bending Tree is his name and a well-earned one at that."

The boulder struck a pose, held up his head, and recited:

*"When storms blow and the earth shakes,
Limber trees may bend, but the stiff will break."*

He relaxed his pose and looked to Skye with one eyebrow cocked. "He's like that, you know, born to be a leader—strong in deeds and decisions, yet not too stiff and set in his ways or traditions, good as they may be.

"You know," Igneous went on, leaning an elbow against a crystal on the wall, "Bending Tree is a pretty great guy, important too. He must not die, my young friend; your mission must not fail. Administer the life-blood of the earth to this man and anyone else that is sick or hurt. It seems that people are always getting hurt, not at all like it used to be before the great flood.

"Speaking of floods, how about we go see that waterfall I told you about?" Igneous spun about and headed out the sapphire doorway, anxious, it seemed, to get to the water.

Skye followed closely behind, wondering what could be more important right now than rescuing this man. Something peculiar was going on.

When they turned the corner out of Hope's grotto, the sound of rushing water echoed down the corridor.

"Ah, here we are." Igneous scrubbed his stony hands together.

Up ahead, water shot out of the mountain through a large, diamond-lined hole. Shafts of sunlight fragmented through the diamond's prisms in the bright colors of the rainbow. The waves of refracted light bounced from crystal to crystal and lit a good portion of the tunnels throughout the mountain. Skye shaded his eyes as he approached. To his right, a spring boiled up and out of a tunnel, and glided over a bed of living-stones that shimmered and flashed in random colors.

"This is one of the seven water-light towers that I told you about. Misty's pretty picky, you know? He finds only the freshest of waters and this water is the best water in the world. In case you want to know, it's 'perfect' water. It has never been tasted before, or touched or tainted by any living thing. The freshest of fresh, the purest of pure, clean and totally …" He gasped as Skye swirled his dirty hands in the beckoning waters. "… unspoiled." Igneous barely finished the sentence. He took a deep breath and continued reluctantly. "Quite all right, master Skye, go right ahead." An unnatural smile pulled across his stony face. "Drink from it, too." He swallowed hard. "If you wish."

Skye didn't think twice. He plunged his whole head into the water and flung it out like a whip, spraying his wet hair back before taking a long drink.

By this time, Igneous had braced himself against the wall. "Delicious?" he squeaked out politely.

"Oh yeah." Skye smiled and slid to the ground with a sigh.

Igneous rolled to the water, bent over, and sniffed. "Ahhh." He looked relieved. "Swept all away, good as new. No harm done."

When Skye went to see what Igneous was talking about, he noticed the sun high in the sky. "Igneous! The morning is getting late. Why are we still here? We should be on our way."

A serious look cracked across Igneous' face. "You're right, it is time. Time to start the wheels in motion." He rolled back and forth rapidly, and rattled off, "Time to weep, time to laugh. Time to plant, time to reap. Time to love, time to—"

The mountain rumbled.

Igneous stopped short and snapped a quick look out the hole then back to Skye. "Time's up. *Sooo* ..." He brushed imaginary dirt from his hands. "... best be moving along." He paused for a moment, and held a hand out. "Well?"

Skye stood, but didn't know what Igneous was referring to.

"Don't just stand there, young man." He extended his hand further, snapping his stony fingers. "Give me your clothes."

Skye hesitated, finally remembering the words Igneous had whispered to him earlier. "Now?"

"Yes, now." *Snap–snap.* Igneous' fingers sounded like rocks banging together.

"Here?"

"Yes, here." *Snap–snap.*

"E-ve-ry-thing?" Skye said.

"Of course, e-ve-ry-thing." The rocky fingers snapped again. "Quickly, my modest man, time's wasting and they'll think you strange enough as it is. It's best you look the part when you drop in."

Snap–snap.

Skye twisted his mouth in thought then turned around, kicked off his boots, and unbuttoned his shirt. He peeked over his shoulder and saw Igneous still looking at him with his hand outstretched. "Could you please? ..." he asked, twirling his finger in a circle. "You're making me nervous."

"Nervous? Why, nothing to be nervous about." Igneous rolled closer. "Seen everything this world has to offer and then some. No need to be nervous around me, no sir. Why, in only the last one hundred years I—"

"*Igneous.*" Skye shot him a panicked glare.

"I'm turning around … I'm rolling away," he said, and settled about ten feet from Skye. "I'm waiting." Impatient fingers clicked against the crystal wall.

One-by-one, articles of clothing sailed over and landed at Igneous' feet. The guardian didn't waste any time. He took the garments and ripped them into calculated sections; fiber fragments floated to the cobbled floor.

"Here, put this on," Igneous said.

A small, rag-like article flew over his stony shoulder and landed at Skye's bare feet. He reached down and held up two pieces of cloth joined together by a strand of leather stripped from his boot.

"Around your waist it goes, my modest friend, no time to lose," Igneous said before Skye asked.

Remnants of cloth still floated to the floor as Igneous continued to rip, knot and tie. Before Skye could fasten his newly fashioned garment, Igneous spun around and held out the last article like a prize.

"Ta-da!"

The guardian took a living-stone from the water, stroked it as if it were a pet, then placed the stone in the sling he'd made and handed it to Skye. "Your time has come, my scantily-clad fellow. Take this down to the village. When you get there, you will know what to do." He placed the sling around Skye's head, and strapped across his chest so it rested over his opposite arm, where it hung like a side bag.

"Word has it from Misty that one of these stones can make a mean bowl of soup. Particularly if you add fresh game, roots, berries, and a smaaall pinch of oregano."

"Oregano?" Skye had never heard of the word.

"Ah, oregano, you say? Funny you should ask—"

The mountain stirred again.

Igneous acknowledged the quake and shot a glance outside. "Oh my, forget the oregano. Why didn't you tell me time was getting on?"

"But I—"

An upheld hand stopped Skye's protest. "You must be off, my dear man. The sun is on the rise, and the Chief is nearly kaput. But not to worry, this is going to be good. Wait 'til the last minute, I always say, that way you get a better reaction. It sticks solid in the mind; it inspires songs and stories to be written."

Igneous snatched another stone from the water and handed it to him. "Come now, master Skye. Let's get you loaded with another healing-stone. That's what the villagers are going to call them, you know. Not a bad name, I might add. However, we prefer living-stone, because they really are 'alive'. They're willing to give their lives for a good cause.

"This other stone must be given to the chief for safekeeping so he and the rest of his people will always remember the miracle that happened this day."

Skye took the stone and placed it in the sling with the first. "I'm ready. We must speed along to the outside cave, if you could lead the way."

"Speed? Why yes, my anxious diplomat," Igneous placed a hand on Skye's upper arm. "I bid you eagle's speed. May the wind be at your back and beneath your wings. Dress warm," he looked skeptically over Skye's new attire. "Get lots of rest and plenty of fluids. Keep your nose clean and for goodness sake, man, get some decent clothes, would you?"

Without warning, the hand on Skye's arm squeezed and lifted him off the ground.

"Hey!" Skye kicked thin air.

With his other hand, Igneous grabbed Skye's ankle and held him dangerously high.

"What are you doing? Let go of me!" Skye thrashed unsuccessfully in Igneous' granite grip.

"Remember when we talked about trust? Well, my feisty fellow, this is the time to start trusting. Trust is a hard thing to do—trust me. However, time has simply run out.

"Speed, my friend. Time is of the essence." His voice thundered. "You must fly."

Skye twisted about, trying to break his hold.

"You must run!" Igneous' earthen voice escalated until it shook the cave. "You must swim!"

"Swim?" Skye panicked, and beat at the arm that held him tight. "But I ca—"

With that last disturbing thought, Igneous tossed Skye headlong into the water, and it swept him away, past the diamonds, through the hole, and out into the day.

Chapter 5
Wet and Wild

The current pulled Skye under. Diamond edges sliced him across his chest and upper leg. Pain gripped him and he inhaled water as he fell from the cliffs of Misty, flailing in a hundred-foot free-fall.

Igneous strained to look out of the water-light tower. "Oh my, hmm. Should have warned him." He yelled out the opening, "Hold your breath!"

Skye plunged into a water-carved pool halfway down the face of the mountain. The impact knocked out the remaining air in his lungs and momentarily paralyzed him. Before he regained his senses, the force of falling water pushed him back under, then up over the edge of the pool, and down the rocky slope where it gushed out of control.

He slammed against boulders, tumbled over rocks, and bounced down a slippery slope of certain death. He had little hope of survival and he felt foolish at being tricked again. Had he not learned anything the day before when rocks pelted him off the mountainside and landed him at the entrance to Igneous' cave?

Maybe, he fumed, *he's the three-legged Thing.*

Death held Skye in its grip again. He continued to tumble and fell into waters that spilled from other water-light towers. Eventually the river swallowed him up and sent him racing along the rapids, fighting for every breath. His life became but a speck in the turbulence and he hoped he'd wake from this nightmare safe in the arms of his wife. She was all he saw before he sailed over the last waterfall and crashed into the lake.

A minute passed before Skye popped up from the pounding waters, spinning on his stomach toward the center of the lake.

I can't swim, he confronted Igneous in his mind.

Too beat-up and too exhausted to reach for another breath of air, he stared hopelessly into the depths of the lake, welcoming death. Without hope, he couldn't hold on anymore, not even for Pearl or his daughter.

In his last heartbeats, he watched fish swimming around leafy plants at the bottom of the lake and wished he could be a fish. He drifted in lazy circles until he floated over a deep, dark nothingness: a hole ripped from the world, an endless abyss of night. It held him there, spinning in place. He thought of nothing as he waited to die, and his lungs filled with water.

As he relaxed in death's grip, something formed in the depths of the abyss. It grew in size and rose with speed toward him. He laughed to himself, thinking yet another catastrophe was about to add its final insult. He embraced his fate and gave up on life, passed out and remembered no more.

The rippling form rushed to the surface, growing in size like a monstrous head pushing through the water for a breath of air. A huge bubble broke the surface, swallowed Skye, and shot him high into the air where he drifted, rocking safely within its fragile skin.

"Good shot again, if I do say so myself!" Igneous cheered as he peered out from the cavern above. "Your aim *is* getting better, isn't it? You never cease to amaze me."

"And you never cease to put me in positions where I have to act on nearly impossible situations." Misty seemed put-out, but secretly enjoyed the satisfying moment of a rescue. "I have him secured for now, but I'm afraid his will to live is not as strong as we once thought."

"Yes, I've noticed. Maybe the stones can help where Hope cannot. It won't be the same effect, but it's his only hope … so to speak."

Igneous placed his elbows on the side of the diamond-studded opening and rested his chin in the cup of his stony hands, watching Skye drift by as the bubble carried him in no particular direction. Igneous drew a long breath until the matrix lines that split around the stones of his body widened with colored light. He held it for a moment then blew steadily until the bubble slowly wobbled in the direction of the village.

"Safe travels, my valiant friend," he said. "Our ways are different, I know, but that's where trust comes in— and you're doing well, yes. Very well indeed."

He filled his lungs again and blew once more.

In the hollow of the bubble, beat and bloodied, Skye

lay at death's door, with the stones in the sling beneath his body. They sensed his condition and acted instinctively. Their purring deepened and a vaporous balm seeped from their shell into the bubble, saturating the atmosphere. Skye still didn't move. One of the stones jumped beneath him, slamming into his chest. His body heaved with the stone, but fell still against the bubble.

Again, the stone jumped.

Nothing.

Harder it thrust … again, then again.

No response.

The other stone followed suit, both of them pitching Skye's body like bacon frying in a pan. While his body flopped about, the stones whined in urgency for his life. Finally, water spewed from his mouth. He gasped, taking in a gurgling breath of medicinal air. Satisfied, the stones stopped and purred soothingly.

In coughing fits, Skye spit more water and blood from his mouth. His jaw quivered and hung open in pain— several teeth fell out. He sunk his hands into the bubble's skin, pushed himself to his knees, and coughed until he thought his lungs would come up. After a few more ragged breaths, the enhanced atmosphere eased his breathing.

He tried to look beyond his eyelids, but could only see with one eye. In his other eye, a stabbing pain almost made him pass out. With trembling fingers, he reached into the lumpy mess of a gouged-out socket. In shock, he fell against the bubble, swinging back and forth like a baby in a cradle. That's when he noticed his position above the earth. Everywhere he looked, he saw …

everything! Even through the pain, he thought it incredible as he floated with the wind. For a brief moment, he forgot about his situation and sank back into the bubble. He tried to gather his thoughts and wondered just how badly he was injured.

A glimpse of his cabin came into view far below. His heart skipped a beat and he tried to stand to see his home, but it was too late—he and the bubble sunk out of sight over the eastern ridge of Elysium.

Skye knelt, exhausted, hurt, and lonely. He wanted to go home. He struck the skin of his cage with his fist, but it only gave way and sprang back.

Just then, an eagle flew over him, wobbling the bubble in its wake and sending Skye backwards against the shell. A second eagle flew under the bubble, its turbulence swinging it the other way. The first eagle circled back and crossed in a different direction. Curious, the two giant birds kept flying near and around the strange anomaly.

Within his capsule, swinging and sliding, Skye's blood smeared the walls of his fragile fortress.

"Whoa. Stop it." he yelled to the eagles. With every pass they made, Skye swung and spun in the bubble. The closer they flew, the more curious they became, and their wings brushed the bubble's surface. Skye swore they enjoyed watching him spin in his rubbery cage. Nauseous, he slapped at the bubble's surface. "Stop it!"

One of the eagles grazed its back against the underside, which sent the bubble—and Skye—in a few complete loops. While the bubble flipped, it drifted, and as it drifted it descended steadily over the upper rim of Elysium and down the steep slope. With the eagles in playful pursuit, the bubble headed for the Anasazi Village on the other side of the Misty River.

The morning sun reflected through the river and off the bed of gold which lined it as naturally as normal stones would. Skye shielded his one eye from the glare and saw children playing and others fishing with spears at its shore.

The bubble skimmed the top of a tree and bounced, sending Skye forward into the bubble's side. The eagles grazed the bubble's top and it skipped off the trees again. The birds took turns in their play on the flight to the river's edge, bouncing Skye in his floating cage over the rushing water.

The transparent ball rolled across the trees of the forest, careening ever closer to the village. He lay on his stomach, trying to control his nausea. Native eyes stared up at him, mouths agape, as he twirled in the bubble.

The people, busy at their work, stopped to investigate the incoming squall. Women screamed and ran; some men bowed in worship while the children cheered.

Right when Skye felt the nausea and dizziness at its peak, an eagle snagged his talon in the floating skin. With a great explosion, the bubble burst and snapped down under Skye's body. The surrounding trees shook, and the people of the village shuddered under its force.

"*Noooo!*" Skye screamed, and his bright world went black.

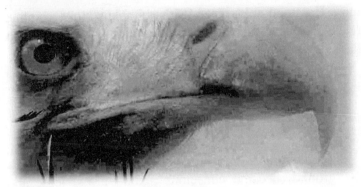

Chapter 6
Do Drop In

The sound of eagles rose above the voices of the people engaged in the ritual inside the wooden hut. Drums, singing, dancing—all stopped. Bewildered expressions spread across their faces, but only one man dared to venture outside.

He pushed the heavy blanket aside from the door, his feathered head leading the way into the sun-streaked courtyard. A trail of smoke from the central fire pointed to the incoming flight of eagles and a strange floating object.

The man stood tall, observing the situation. An explosion ripped the sky. It shook the trees and blew the flame out in the pit. A spray of liquid, followed by a large object, splattered before him, and a nearly-naked white man landed in the middle of it all.

In the sky, two eagles scattered like children caught doing something they shouldn't have done.

For a moment the woods were silent. The man with the feathered headdress remained calm. He pondered the situation briefly then walked with purpose to the fallen man. He stood ankle-deep in the bubble's slimy residue, reached over and poked the semiconscious newcomer in the side with his rattling stick.

"You," he said with authority. "You fell from Misty's sky."

Skye, having momentarily blacked out when he'd hit the ground, became conscious again—arms, legs, and head flailing about as if he were a turtle trying to right himself. He searched frantically for the force behind the probing stick and the voice that commanded it.

His focus found a man wearing a headdress of feathers that fanned to his shoulders. Paint striped his face, and bells and beads hung at his waist and ankles, and rattled every time he moved. And he moved a lot. Back and forth on bubble slime he paced, then he leaned over and prodded Skye.

"You!"

Skye flinched with each poke and the living-stone's purr turned into a growl.

The medicine man stood straight and peered at the jumping sling hanging at Skye's side.

Skye didn't know why, or how, he just knew the stones were calling him to his mission. He wasn't sure he wanted to answer the call—he was wounded on purpose, manipulated, and deeply offended at the abuse.

Fool me once, shame on you. Fool me twice ... He cringed at the truth to the proverb. ... *Shame on me.* "And I," Skye said through broken teeth, "have become a fool." Blood spewed from his mouth with the words.

His body had been so battered that bruises were already evident. The cuts on his chest and upper leg stung, and the damage to his eye was beyond repair—it was gone. He struggled to stand on the bubble's skin, swayed painfully on his bleeding feet, and the stones jumped in the sling at his side. Skye put a careful hand to his gaping eye socket and glared with contempt at the mountain. An angry breath wheezed past his lips. "I won't—be—fooled—again!"

He took the sling from his neck, dropped it to the slimy ground, turned, and hobbled away. Every step felt like walking on broken glass. He took no notice of the people who gathered to see what they thought was the birth of a white man from the sky. He took no notice of the surrounding beauty or the songbirds whistling cheerful tunes. He took no notice of the stones whose voices now sounded like the deep-sea cries of singing whales. He simply wanted out.

Go back home, he tried to convince himself. *Forget everything. Go home.*

"You!" The medicine man roared again, rattling his stick at Skye. *"You fell from Misty's sky."*

In rhythmic beats, his foot pounded the bubble's blubbery skin. He closed his eyes, craned his neck up, and sang an ancient song:

> *"When days of old and troubles pass by*
> *A man shall fall from Misty's sky*
> *Rocks and stones shall bite his bones,*
> *And death be near his side;*
> *A secret found where once thought dead,*
> *Stones that bleed in green, not red.*
> *It mends the hurt and clears the mind;*
> *It puts what's right back into time.*
> *White as snow yet pure as gold,*
> *A man you've never seen*

Shall bring to you a rocky stew
With life that's ever green."

Skye froze in his tracks and listened to the song. What he heard took him by surprise. He turned around. It wasn't the song as much as the fact that he understood every word. He also heard the sporadic conversation of the people, spoken in their own language, completely foreign to him. But he wholly understood it—all of it.

His skin prickled.

"Did you see the man in the floating womb?" Skye heard one woman ask another.

"What is he doing? Is he going to be okay?" an older woman asked.

Skye shuffled backwards; frightened by knowing a language he'd never heard before.

"No, all I heard was the explosion," another explained to a friend.

Skye glanced about, picking up conversations here and there over the purring of the stones.

"A prophecy fulfilled," an excited citizen proclaimed.

"A warrior comes to warn us!"

Skye continued his backward retreat, looking about.

"The sky ripped open and cast this man from heaven," a father told his son.

When Skye moved further away from the stones, the comments became muffled.

"No, h- wasn't c-st from h-aven," the man's wife said, "he c-me f-om hea-en."

A few steps farther and the translations ceased. Only the unfamiliar mumbles of an unknown language remained. Skye stopped to think about the change and his gaze rested on the stones. Curious, he took a few staggering steps forward.

"I s-w ev-rything—the sun g-ve birth to a son!"

The translations had come back—weak, but back. A few steps more and they became strong again.

"You!" the medicine man bellowed across the court. "You fell from Misty's sky. At last, you have come." He waved everyone back with his stick.

Skye didn't answer because he couldn't speak—his energy nearly spent. He was crazy to think he could walk away without medical treatment and rest.

He wobbled, weak from blood loss and pain, and his head spun in dizzy circles. He needed help, and fast. His eye fixed on the jumping sling—his only salvation.

The chatter of the crowd echoed in his ears, but all he could think was that the stones had power. They were the only thing left to trust. Igneous had designed them to help, and right now he needed help. Try as he might, his legs wouldn't obey. Total hopelessness overtook him and he sank to his skinned knees.

The painted man snagged and lifted the sling of jumping stones with his rattling stick. He leaned over and peeked into the pouch, sniffing. The tone of the stones changed and the man looked as though he understood something. He stood, and stared directly at Skye. Without hesitation, he carried the sling on his stick and placed it on the ground in front of Skye.

"Misty has spoken of you. You are the one."

Skye's heart beat wildly—the stones were within his reach. He took one from the sling and felt the power surge from its core. With both hands, he struggled to lift it before feebly thrusting it to the ground.

It didn't break.

Again, he fought to raise the stone, then drove it back to the earth.

It still didn't break.

Sweat dripped from his brow, stinging his good eye. In desperation he struggled again—arms trembling, voice groaning—to lift the beckoning stone to save his life.

Strong hands grabbed hold of his. With the help of the painted man, together, they lifted the stone high, and with a mighty thrust they slammed it hard against the ground, splitting the oracle in two.

It purred no more.

Thick, teal liquid oozed from the stone and Skye breathed in the comforting spicy scent. He scooped his fingers into the liquid, then tipped his head back and slathered the ointment directly into his eye socket.

Instantly, a tingling sensation enveloped the area. Something pulled within the cavity. It made him sigh as if it were an itch finally getting a much-needed scratch. He cupped the area with a hand, feeling a pulling and stretching inside the socket until it pushed against the eyelid where it came to rest. The socket grew warm and the pain vanished. Skye blinked open a new eye.

Chatter exploded within the crowd of people—they had just witnessed a miracle. But Skye needed more healing.

He reached again into the stone, and smeared the elixir across his chest and upper thigh where deep gashes revealed muscle tissue. Seconds later—as if stitching from the inside out—the wounds closed. His shredded feet were next. They, too, stitched up with new skin.

Skye jumped to his restored feet and looked up to the mountain, remembering everything. His pain had purpose. Skye took the stone from the painted man, held high his salvation, and shouted: "To Misty and the guardian of the mountain, I give thanks."

He put his mouth to the stone and drank. Cuts and bruises all over his body vanished. He stopped and put a hand to his mouth, which made him look as though he were gagging, then spit broken teeth to the ground. When he removed his hand, a smile revealed new teeth. Then something else happened: energy—lots of it—coursed through him. In the middle of a jump, he shouted. From the looks he got from the people, songs and stories would be sure to follow.

The medicine man wasted no time. In one hand he carried the shell, and with the other he grabbed Skye by the arm and towed him across the common area. The people followed close behind. "You are the chosen one."

Chapter 7
Chief Bending Tree

The medicine man pulled Skye straight toward a hogan hut: a round house made of sticks and thatched with mud. Skye noticed something and pulled back. He had been here before. Or had he?

"You must come." Skye's escort pulled at his wrist.

Skye ignored the man. Everything in the village—the trees, the huts, even the dogs playing, felt familiar. He remembered the vision with Igneous and knew exactly what to expect inside this particular hut.

"Bending Tree," Skye whispered.

"Bending Tree." The man took Skye's arm.

Skye grabbed the stone's half-shell from him and plunged into the hut. The drummer stopped and a woman fixed wide, teary eyes on him. They had never seen a white person, let alone one with blond hair.

Skye recognized the pregnant woman from the vision. Near her, a bowl burned incense. Ornaments lined the walls of the hut, befitting a man of great stature—a pipe, a bow and arrow, an obsidian-tipped spear, and a large, feathered headdress. Below these, on a bearskin, lay the wounded chief himself. In one hand the chief held a knife hewn from stone. His other hand lay mangled on his chest beside five gaping holes over his heart.

Skye stepped forward and knelt beside him while the medicine man rattled his stick softly.

"Bending Tree, the Mountain brings you a gift." Skye dipped his hand into the stone, took hold of the chief's shredded hand and got to his feet. "Be well," he said. Then he pulled the chief to his feet.

The chief stood uneasily, his eyes fluttered open, and returned a fuzzy gaze.

The pregnant woman screamed. The drummer ran to defend their leader, but the outstretched arm of the medicine man intercepted him. "Sit and be still," he ordered. "This white man is the chosen one."

The drummer, knowing the prophecy, bowed his head and retreated.

Skye couldn't believe he had just pulled a dying man from his deathbed. *What in the world did I just do?*

Swiftly, unexpectedly, the chief twisted Skye's hand behind his back then swept the stone knife against his neck. Skye again wondered: *What in the world did I just do?*

"Death," the chief said, still delirious, "you come again for me at last. If you sing, I will cut your throat."

The knife pricked Skye's skin and his eyes widened. The healing stone outside was still close enough to translate, and Skye understood that once again he was in serious trouble. He swallowed hard against the blade. "Sing?" he said through a tight smile. "I'm not all that bad, really."

The chief brought his face closer. "Cruel are your weapons, but my life is not over. Today is my day to live, not yours." He threw Skye to the door and pointed with his knife. "Go now or die."

The medicine man lowered the hand that held the knife. "You are safe, my chief. The Legend has come alive, not Death."

Bending Tree blinked as if he'd woken from a dream. He shook his head and placed a hand over the wounds on his chest. While struggling to sit back down, he beckoned Skye closer with his knife. "You are the one who falls from Misty?"

Skye nodded.

"We prayed for you to come and waited even in death for you." He extended his healed hand. "Fulfill your destiny."

Skye took the broken stone from the ground and held it out to the chief. "Drink."

Unsteady hands took the stone. The chief didn't hesitate to drink, and his face relaxed as he swallowed the elixir.

The wrinkles on the chief's aged face disappeared, his hair took on a darker hue, and flowed about his broad shoulders as if alive. He drew a deep breath, the holes in his chest glowed, and the festered wounds gradually squeezed down into five pinholes then disappeared completely, leaving the skin unmarred.

He jumped to his feet, quivering with energy, and thrust his knife three times into the air. "Whoa–whoa–whoa!" he shouted.

Skye's face lit up. "Remedy-rush." He chuckled. "So that's what it looks like."

Bending Tree clapped Skye's shoulders and squeezed reassuringly. "Welcome to the home of my people," he said, smiling. "Our home is your home."

The pregnant woman pushed in and threw her arms

around the chief's neck. "Husband, you are well!"

Bending Tree picked her up from the ground and carefully swung her around. "Kwanita, my heart sings. It has been so long I have forgotten your face." He held her hands, observing her condition. "You have changed."

Kwanita giggled and placed his hand on her swollen belly. "Our child grows each day, my husband. He kicks hard, like a pony, to let me know he wants to see his father … alive." She pushed her finger into Bending Tree's side, tickling him.

Kwanita gasped and pulled away to cradle her unborn. She smiled. "Kicks like a pony."

"Like a pony," Bending Tree said. "Pony." He nodded his head. "Pony. Our child's name shall be Pony!"

"Yes, Pony is a good name, my husband. Good for one who kicks so well. May our child run just as swiftly."

They laughed and kissed until the chief's face became serious. He pointed the knife to the medicine man's painted face and shook his head. "Yenene, you don't look so well—a little pale, yes? Go see the medicine man," he pointed with a flick of his chin and grinned. "He will rattle his stick and sing, and smear paint over you until the chosen one comes."

They shared a look then burst into laughter.

"Whoa–whoa–whoa!" The chief thrust his knife into the air again then pulled the door rug aside and ran through with the others close behind. Outside, the people looked puzzled at the man with paint smeared on his chest and face.

"Whoa–whoa–whoa!" Bending Tree danced around the people, making his way to the second stone in the middle of the bubble's slimy skin. He took the healing-stone, and swung it around as he danced.

"My people." Bending Tree shouted. "Why do you look frightened? Your Chief is healed—rejoice." He held the stone in the air and continued his dance.

"Whoa–whoa–whoa." The people, finally recognizing him, echoed the jubilant cry and danced with him. They pulled Skye along, and caught up in their celebration, he joined in, dancing to the beat of their song.

The celebration evolved into food—lots of it. Venison with herbs, pine nuts, and the remaining blood of the stone boiled in a pot over the common fire. As the festivities progressed, the scent filled the air with energy. People dipped freely into the green stew, and as they ate, happiness came over them.

Skye laughed, remembering something Igneous had said. "Oregano," he shouted, "does anyone have oregano?"

Chapter 8
Soul Stalker

In spite of his increasing anxiety to be home, Skye decided to stay a few days more to become better acquainted with Bending Tree and his people. Skye carried the last living-stone in the sling around his neck so it could interpret while he and the chief talked. They spoke of many things concerning Misty and, as they walked the hillside, Skye asked a pressing question. "What happened to you before I came? Were you attacked?" He shaded his eyes with one hand and pointed to the rocky face of the volcano with the other. "When I walked in Misty's caverns, Igneous showed me a vision of you in the hogan but never told me what caused your wounds or who rescued you. It looked as if a bear got hold of you."

"A bear walks on all fours," Bending Tree said. "A bear would have been merciful. No one had encountered a thing like this before."

"Did you see it?"

"It was …" he fought for the words, "… beauty with claws."

"A mountain lion?"

"No. A mountain lion walks on all fours and its kill would also be merciful. This creature showed no mercy. I was helpless in its play, and it played cruelly."

Skye picked nervously at his fingernails while Bending Tree recalled the encounter.

"It was more human than animal. Colored stones formed its body and it smelled of sulfur. It stank of evil, but sang with beauty, as if it were a good spirit."

Troubled by the words, Skye stopped and sat on a rock, adjusting the sling to his lap.

"It glowed like a magnificent light, but it smothered like darkness." Bending Tree turned and looked at Skye. "It … it sang to my soul."

Skye remembered something similar, right before the clouds had hit him several days before.

The chief's eyes darted back and forth as if reliving the encounter. "It ran … no, it walked. It walked swiftly on—"

"Three legs." Skye nodded.

"Yes, three gem-coated legs." Bending Tree glanced sideways to Skye. "You have seen it?"

"No." Skye stared at the ground, remembering. "I'm sure I heard it, though. It was as you said, beautiful and captivating. I thought of nothing else when I heard it. It came close to getting me, too." He tried to shake the image from his head. "The guardian of the mountain spoke of a recent intruder in the cavern. He said it walks on three legs. It destroyed hundreds of living-stones just to hear them scream. The guardian was quite upset."

Skye brushed his hair out of his eyes. "We don't have to talk about it if you don't want to," he said, putting a hand to Bending Tree's shoulder.

"No, our legend said Misty would send you to us for a

reason. I think it's best you know about the thing that stalks our woods."

He took a cleansing breath then told his story. "On the north side of Misty where the boulders meet with the trees, I went to pay tribute to our first ancestors, White Bear and Snow Moon. They were the first to come to this mountain long ago. It is a story told from father to son to his son's children. We sing songs to keep their legend alive, burning in our hearts. Most believe in these stories, but some refused to—until you came.

"Their gravestones are carved from unknown ancient hands. I went to pray and sing the Song of Passing as I always do this time of year. When I arrived, I found the sacred place dishonored. The grave markers had been broken and scratched, as if by a bear. I tried to lift them back in place, but could not."

The chief settled onto a rock next to Skye. He stretched his arms over his knees, closed his eyes, and recounted the event. "I sang and danced my respect to them anyway. Then many sounds singing in the air interrupted me. Like a hundred flutes … no, voices. Voices so rich, so beautiful, they captured my soul as they sang.

"I turned to see, but I found nothing. From the forest where the music came, something small flashed in midair, then vanished. Something else small appeared about this high." He held a flat hand to his shoulder. "It was shiny, and as big as a bird, but not a bird. Then it disappeared. Then a silver piece appeared lower, this high." He dropped his hand to his knees. "Then it vanished. Another ragged piece flashed. Then another here, here, and here." He moved his hands to different spots, and then clapped them together. "Gone, like that. Again and again, pieces flashed and disappeared.

"Its music trapped my mind as the pieces drew closer, and I realized they were fitting together in the shape of a man. Yellow smoke danced to its music as many parts of the creature appeared and disappeared. The smell of sulfur grew strong. As frightened as I was, I could not move. Then the music stopped and my heart ached with the silence—I never wanted the music to end."

He turned to face Skye. "I could not believe what was happening. I wanted to hear the voices over and over again, but they were taken away like a child from its mother's arms."

The chief's eyes grew glassy. He glanced away and cleared his throat before continuing. "I heard uneven footsteps approaching as the creature came closer. It terrified me. Somehow I found the will to turn away, but its clawed hand grabbed my shoulder, cutting deep as it forced me around. Then thunder shot like burning arrows through my chest. I looked down and saw jeweled fingers knuckle-deep over my heart. The pain was so great, I had to cry out."

The chief's voice cracked. He scooted off the rock and paced back and forth, looking at the treetops and blinking back tears. "I am humiliated," he said at last. "Men do not scream as I did. I pulled at the hand and beat the arm that held me. It only brought more pain—torture so cruel that I longed to die. A bear would have been merciful, but not this … this thing. I hated it. And it thrived on my hate.

"I could not stop thrashing in its grip, and my throat became raw from screaming. I yelled over and over for it to stop. Why would it do this to me?

"Its head appeared, hidden under a silver hood. I saw eyes within it through wisps of smoke—silver eyes that sparkled wickedly. I sensed I was teaching it my deepest fear and it absorbed it through my heart. I could do nothing but surrender to its evil curiosity."

The chief sat back down and put his head between his hands. "It was not satisfied. It wanted more than the screaming, so it arched me back in its grip. Its fingers burned hot, pushing deeper until its palm lay against my chest, burning my flesh as it went. I felt my heart beating against its ragged nails. I dangled from its fist like a doll in the hands of a child and prayed for death to take me. That's when it released its grip, dropping me over my ancestor's grave. It seemed satisfied with what it learned, and left me to die. I was barely alert. The last thing I remember is that it retreated back into the shadows of the woods. I am sure—it walked on three legs."

Bending Tree clapped his hand on Skye's shoulder and stood. A smile tried to overpower his frightened face. "The next thing I remember is you in the healing lodge."

The two shared many things that day. Skye spoke of his adventure in the mountain, describing his visit with the rock-man named Igneous. He also spoke of his journey across the ocean and his flight to the other side of the mountain to live with his wife and child. As he spoke, he longed to be with them again—it was time to go home.

On the morning of the third day, Skye made ready to leave. It would be a few days' journey by foot, so the sooner he departed the better.

When he stepped out of his hut, Bending Tree stood holding the reins of a pony in one hand and the purring stone to translate in the other. The beautiful pinto held its head high as the chief handed Skye the reins. "You have stayed long. It is late for your return. He will carry you to your loved ones and some day will bring you back."

Skye hadn't expected this. He was grateful and humbled by the gift and graciously accepted it. "Thank you. I will treat him well and honor our friendship. Someday soon he will carry me here again and we will celebrate." Skye mounted the pony, turned, and trotted west out of camp.

Bending Tree's face seemed happy but his eyes betrayed the sadness in his heart as Skye rode away.

Children appeared one by one from behind trees as Skye passed by. They said their goodbyes with flowers and trinkets they'd made from leather and wood. He took their gifts and ruffled a few heads. With a parting wave, he loped out of sight. A part of him would always remain with the people, but in a couple of days he'd be back in Pearl's arms where he belonged, and with many strange stories to tell.

Two days later, as the morning sun streaked golden rays across the tree tops, Skye rode into the dew-washed meadow around his cabin.

On a stump outside his home, Pearl sat staring up at the mountaintop with their child cradled in her arms.

His horse reared and sang out a whinny, breaking the stillness of the moment. Pearl turned and watched him gallop towards her. She stood and walked forward, straining her eyes to see. A smile grew on her face and she rushed forward.

Butterflies scattered in a bouquet of colors as Skye dismounted to receive her embrace—he was home.

"Very nice, if I do say so myself, very nice indeed. Don't you think, Misty?"

"Yes, my old friend. Well done, and so ends the first stage."

"Yes, all is now ready to start."

Chapter 9
Unexpected Visitors

Far off on a distant continent—where tempers burned hot and hearts grew cold with the wind—a fever broke out. For centuries, this fever caused men to pillage, covet, and war. The fever germinated in their minds, cultivated itself in their hearts, and planted its seed deep within many generations of their children. They rationalized 'bad' as being 'good' and 'wrong' as 'right.' They justified their pleasure and it kept the fever burning shamelessly in their souls.

The fever had a name, but the people refused to recognize its true title—greed. It hadn't yet sunk its infectious fangs into Misty's clean world, but it was more than ready to spread, and it would have its way.

In the plains far from Misty, stories arose of a treasure beyond price. A stone that lives was said to be more lustrous than gold and worth more than diamonds. This treasure, above all treasures, would restore health and youth forever. How and where they heard of it, no one could say; they just knew it would be found somewhere on Mount Misty—the name foreigners called the single volcanic peak that towered over a sea of rolling hills.

So crazy was greed's momentum that even wealthy prospectors, rich from their earlier mining, pulled up stakes when they heard the rumor, and they took their place in the cold winter march to Misty. On foot and horseback, a horde of hardened men, hundreds, trickled into a river of treasure-seekers splattered with freezing mud. They weren't willing to wait for the spring thaw, fearful that someone might beat them to a claim.

The throng made its way to the mountain, where it exploded like shrapnel against the lower skirts of the volcano. In a few short months, camps and random diggings littered the countryside. Settlers marked their territory and took root, scouts explored, and emotions ran high. Fights and murders were everyday events. They scarred the land in their fruitless search for the treasure above all treasures—the elusive fountain of youth.

Misty showed signs of unrest, quivering as the invaders ventured nearer to the village under his protection. So great was the horde of intruders that Misty wondered if he'd be able to shield his people from the plundering.

On this morning, the dawn's light hid in a blanket of gray clouds that threatened to drop more snow. While Misty engaged in counsel with Igneous, two men approached the village. From the dark woods, an undernourished horse carried a tall, lanky rider wearing a cold stare. A disheveled tub of a man, riding a mangy mule, followed him in. The two men meandered into the camp as if they owned it.

Both wore identical attire: tawny, mud-splattered pants and black, tattered sea coats over blousy white-sleeved shirts and buttoned vests. Their gray woolen scarves were thick enough for the frigid air, but their low-top leather shoes were fashioned more for the hard wooden decks of a ship than for the rocky mountain terrain. Their clothes and wind-burned faces spoke of their lives on the sea. The only difference in their attire was their hats—the taller man had one, the squatty man did not, revealing a sparsely-haired scalp. The thin, aging man, Erikson, had been the captain of a ship. His younger halfwit crewman, Toby, was the only shipmate willing to tag along with the overbearing and cantankerous captain.

The captain and his sea mate had taken to the trail after hearing news of Misty's riches in the settlement of Pandemonium—a lawless town of gold smelters located a few miles inland by the banks of the Misty River. The two took more information than they gave and stole more than they bought. Their horses and supplies were the fruits of their cheating labor.

On this frigid morning, there had been no warning of their approach. The village children, tending the horses and dogs, ran to their huts while some of the women ran to get their men. The men—some with blankets draped around their shoulders, others with bows or knives—gathered around the unexpected company as the newcomers made their way to the fire in the village center.

Erikson looked piously down on the gathering people, but his eyes betrayed his false smile. "Keep an eye out, Toby," he cautioned out the corner of his mouth in a thick accent.

"Aye, Cap." Toby's gaze darted about. "I be a eyein' 'em all right … with me hand on me pistol—bless da King."

"Good lad. Jus' keep yer smile steady an' things'll be fine."

"Aye, fine as rat's hair," Toby said.

Erikson snapped back on the reins to stop his emaciated horse and shifted in the saddle. The horse thrust its head up to slacken the tension on its bit. Liking his position above the people, Erikson leaned over, his back straight, chin held high, eyes veering down.

"Food fer weary travelers, lads?" he asked sweetly. Tiny icicles swung from his beard. His eyes flicked across the unresponsive faces, then gave a stray look to Toby, who shrugged his thick shoulders. Erikson gazed back down at the people, his voice a little louder, almost a polite bark. "Food, lads?" His smile fell a bit. "Meat?"

Nothing. No response, only the sidelong glances and murmurs of the people around him.

The villagers looked bewildered.

Erikson turned back to Toby, the saddle creaking beneath him.

"Might I be wrong, mate?" Erikson said, looking down at his simpleminded companion who had a fake smile plastered below big, frosty eyebrows. "Either be they a wee bit daft or be they stupid savages of a different tongue." He chuckled at his putdown.

Toby chuckled with him through shivering teeth and eyed the warmth of the blazing fire. "Bless da King."

Erikson turned his attention again to the people. He grabbed the bill of his hat and flipped it off. With his other hand, he made as if he were eating. "Food, ya bloody dumb barbarians," he said with an overly expressive smile. "Be ya bloody deaf as ya are ugly? *Fooood!*"

The natives stared as quietly as the intermittent flakes of snow that fell from the gathering clouds.

Erikson's grin softened with a chuckle, and the vapor of his breath floated in the crisp air. He gave Toby a sideways glance. "Well, I'll be, Toby, me boy!" he shouted over his shoulder to his companion. "Looks like the whole bunch be dumb as you—*bless da King*."

Toby's bright smile faded and his head sank into his frozen gray scarf.

A thick blanket drew back from the doorway of a hut and a man stood for a moment in the falling snow, surveying the situation. He wore ceremonial clothes. His headdress, made of eagle feathers, draped around his head and past his shoulders, and displayed a great quantity and color of feathers. In his hand, he held a long-stemmed pipe adorned with feathers that dangled from strips of colored leather.

"Aye, now," Erikson said with a lift to his voice and brow, "there be someone worthy of me company." He flipped his billed hat back onto his disheveled head of gray-flecked, red hair. "Come, Toby, we's got work ta do."

Stiff, Erikson dismounted his horse. He adjusted his coat around his thin frame and took a few slippery steps on the ground toward a line of people.

"Pardon me, scurvy." He smiled at the first man before him and nudged him aside. With a plastered grin on his face, he tipped his hat and took a few more steps into the crowd. "Comin' through, ya miserable excuses of life," he said, leaning forward and pushing two more aside. He giggled to himself, proud, and enjoying the blunt insults he was getting away with.

He stopped in the middle of them all. His voice rose high, and his hands reached out as if he were giving a welcoming speech to these mountain people. They seemed amused by his actions. "Hear ye, all ye greedy packrats of the mountain. Gluttonous hoarders of the fount'n'o youth." He turned slowly in a full circle as he spoke, giving Toby a wink as he twirled by.

Toby chuckled and dismounted awkwardly from his mule. He waddled over to the fire, and brushed his hands together over the flames.

"Me knows of yer treasure and you's can formally bids it … farewell." Erikson took a deep bow, and caught his hat perfectly by the bill as it slipped from his head. With a grin matching his large ego, he stood up and stared through the ragged aisles of people. Playfully, he shooed the rest away with his hat. "Now outta me way, *dogs!*"

Sporadic, shy chuckles spread among the people while their leader waited, observing the foreign men. His face remained expressionless.

"Toooby," Erikson drawled as he threaded his way to the other side.

Toby, still warming his toes by the fire, jerked alive.

"Aye, Cap." He shuffled in behind.

"Keep *smiiiling*," the captain added, then he wiggled a little dance and skipped for the people before he turned to face their leader, his hand outstretched. "Pleased ta be acquainted with yer filthy treasure." With a tilt of his head, he looked the chief straight in the eye and gave a little bow.

The chief locked eyes with the captain. "What is this, 'filthy treasure'?"

Erikson froze in his animated position. His gaze darted about. He plainly heard the man speak in a language he'd never heard, but somehow he understood it, exactly.

Slowly, he straightened, placing his hat back on his head. His heavy accent was hard enough for most to understand, but the village leader evidently had no problems. The captain's face sobered.

The chief's gaze intensified. "What is this 'fountain of

youth'? And why do you insult my people and say they are greedy, then call them 'dogs'?"

"Fount'n'o youth? Dogs?" Erikson looked around, baffled. His face reddened.

"Dogs?" Toby said in a low monotone as he came skidding to a stop behind the captain. "I likes dogs—bless da King."

Erikson brightened, and turned to put a hand around Toby's thick shoulder, patted the side of his big cheeks with his other hand. "Aye, mate," he said with a sly grin, *"dooogs."*

He crafted a story while straightening Toby's scarf. "Sorry fer the misconception, as it be. In our culture now, dogs be good, ya know?" He cleared his throat. "An' a beaut' of a beast dogs be, ta be sure. Loyal … brave … an' friendly …" He looked around, trying to figure out the purring sound and how he and the chief could understand each other. "Where we comes from, call'n yer good folk here 'dogs' be a compliment. Ya know? Loyal, brave an' friendly like. In't that right, Toby?" Erikson gave an elbow jab to Toby's ribs.

"Aaaaye, Cap." Toby looked bewildered. "Heard da king's got one'o his very own, he do—bless him."

"Oh, he does now, does he?" Erikson gave Toby a sideways glance and chuckled to the chief. "Well there ya go, the king's got a dog. Now if'n that ain't proof, nothin' be."

Then to dodge the "filthy treasure" and "fountain of youth" comments, he stood straight, shoulders back, and introduced himself. "Capt'n Erikson, I be, at yer service … *Dog.*" He spit in his cold hand and extended it out in hopes the story would stick and his derogatory remarks would be forgotten.

"Dog." The chief watched the village dogs playing

with the children and each other. "Dogs are good, yes. It is sometimes our custom to name our people after a worthy animal, like my son, Pony. 'Dog' has never been considered, but we will honor your ways. I am Bending Tree, Chief of the Anasazi people."

Toby and Erikson gave each other a look of relief, though still baffled about the translations—to hear what they couldn't understand, yet understand what they heard, was an eerie experience.

"Please ta make yer acquaintance, Mr. Bendin' ... Chief," Erikson said with a bow. Toby copied him.

Bending Tree's eyes flicked over them, scrutinizing. "Tell me, Erikson dog. Where is the land you come from?"

Erikson's brows pulled together momentarily. Being called 'dog' stung a bit, but he'd started the game and now would have to play along. "Where's we from?" Erikson's eyebrow lifted in question. "Well now, Chief, that be an honest question, ta be sure, ain't it, Toby?"

"Bless—" Toby received another elbow jab to his side. "Aye, Cap."

"Let me see now." The captain pulled back his coat and jerked a long, steel knife from his belt.

The village men moved forward through the crowd, drawing stone knives. Others nocked arrows to their bows. Bending Tree raised a hand, and his men lowered their weapons but kept guarded eyes on the strangers.

Erikson glanced around at the valiant, yet pathetic, savages, pleased at the success of his ploy to find out what primitive weapons he might be facing. He had a pistol in his belt, a musket in its scabbard on his horse, and Toby had a pistol stuffed in the top of his pants. The captain snickered and thought smugly, *If these people only knew what me firearms could do.*

He eyed the people and chuckled, then squatted down and swept the dry flakes from the top of the hard-packed snow. With his steel knife he drew in the snow's crust.

The people stared at the shiny blade; it looked nothing like their primitive stone knives.

The chief held the ends of his bearskin cloak and leaned forward to see what the captain had drawn. He squinted at the lines in the snow, and his braided hair dangled to the sides of his weathered, brown face.

"This here be the sea," Erikson said.

"Yes, long ago I have been to these wide waters," the chief said, pointing to the etched image with his long-stemmed pipe. "To drink it is poison to the tongue."

"Aye, Chief, they be. An' the sea'll poison yer very soul if'n ya be around 'er long 'nough, guaranteed. Gets into yer blood, she do, an' possesses yer mind 'til her sparklin' wavy hair carries ya away to her bottomless bosom." He said it sincerely, with a distant look in his eye. With a sigh, he scratched more lines in the snow.

"Now this here sea separates me home on this here island off'a these coasts by thirty days or more of sailin' the wind." He paused to blow warm air on his fingers. "Terrible place it be fer folks like me growin' up there, ya know." His voice became emotional and he patted Toby's thick ankle. "Been treated most our life, Toby an' I, as slaves, we were. Hungry an' cold—always cold."

Toby added: "Aye, an' forced ta labor at the ports, carryin' cargo without a morsel of food, scrapin' barnacles off'a the hull on empty stomachs, an' beggin' fer apples so's our teeth don't fall out no more … an' swabbin' the ship's deck without drink … an'—"

Erikson cleared his throat and gave Toby a sharp glance. "Sailed the sea most o' me life through these parts here, here, an' here." He made X marks across the coastal waters around his continent then sat back on his heels a moment, wanting to drive a point home.

"Ya know, Bendin' Chief, I's always believed in treatin' me crew better than I be treated as a lad, and chanced the long voyage ta these parts in hopes of findin' peace in the soul fer me and me crew. Anchored me ship fer the last time on these waters by a large river right about … *there*." He sank the knife deep into the packed snow.

The corners of his mouth dropped as he lifted sad eyes to the chief. "Toby 'an me's been wanderin' lost fer months," he said, trying to sound pathetic. "Can't seem ta find our way in this here cold world no more. An' we's be mighty grateful to ya if'n ya can spare some food an' shows us 'round a bit."

He sniffed, wiping his nose with his frozen sleeve, then conjured up wet eyes to exaggerate his need. "If'n ya know anythin' good about the mountain that can soothe me tortured soul or ease our way, we'd be mighty glad of it—anythin', anythin' at all ya can tell us good folk about?"

The captain stood stiffly with upturned hands, pleading. A well-placed tear slid down his thin, sharp nose. His act played good. The months of practicing in Pandemonium were paying off; even Toby added a sniffle and a bow of the head to the captain's trembling words.

Bending Tree contemplated the two, his breath fogged before him in the crisp air. With a wave of his hand, he spoke a word to the buckskin-clad men at his side. One ran off and returned holding a spear wrapped in colored leather and adorned with stones and feathers.

Erikson's eyes grew large at the sight of the glassy, carved obsidian tip. He'd never seen anything so primitive yet so deadly before.

Bending Tree traded his pipe for the spear and the captain's mouth went dry. He nearly fell over backwards watching the sharp tip rise dangerously close to his buttoned coat.

"We know of the many men camping on the outskirts of Misty," the chief said. "They are marking the earth with their tools and fighting among themselves ..." Bending Tree turned the spear and stabbed the map. "... *here*. It is not good for these foreign men to fight on our mountain, to mark its beauty, or to kill." He turned the spear again to the captain, but higher, near his neck. "Also, it is not good for foreign men to call my people 'greedy' and 'hoarders of treasure.'" He gave Erikson a penetrating glare. "Are you one who came to mark our mountain, to steal from Misty that which is good? To kill?"

A lump formed in Erikson's throat. He'd hoped the chief had forgotten about his "greedy" and "hoarder" remarks. "No! We's been runnin' from them crazy folk fer weeks now. They's try robbin' us a time or two, way down past the big bend in the river where the trees meet the plains. We's done them no harm. Fact 'tis," he said with a nervous chuckle, "Toby an' I here, we's come ta help the poor folk in their times of trouble. In't that right, Toby?"

Toby brushed the snow off his head with stubby fingers protruding through tattered wool gloves. "Swears to da King, we do—bless him."

"An' what do we's get's fer our help? Our food an' blankets thieved from us, that's what. Can ya imagine takin' the things we's need ta survive this here cold? Would o' took an' ate me horse an' mule too if'n we hadn't snuck out a couple of nights ago an' raced here ta warn all ya of their terrible ways. Good thing we's got here in time, too. Nice folk ya got here, if'n ya don't mind me tellin'? Mighty nice." He licked his lips. "An' well fed."

Toby wiggled his toes in his frozen black leather shoes and added with a shiver. "An' warm."

Bending Tree seemed satisfied for the moment and planted the butt end of the spear into the snow's crust. "It is not good to judge a tree to be cut down in winter. One must wait for the beauty of its blossoms in spring, and later, the fruit it will bear. In the same way, I will not judge you in your winter months before your fruit is revealed." With both hands, he took each visitor by the shoulders. "Welcome, Captain 'dog,' to our home ... welcome."

Erikson knew with certainty he didn't like the derogatory title, but again, it had been his idea.

The chief had made his point clear. He pulled the heavy rug back from the hut's doorway. "Come, there is food and warmth inside."

"Aye," the captain rubbed his hands together, "now ya be talkin'."

"Bless da king," Toby muttered.

The two visitors ducked into the peace lodge, a place for making important decisions, for counseling tribal members, and an honored place for guests. The scent of spice eddied through the air, refreshing the minds of all. With the spiced air came the comforting sound of the purring stone. It had a soothing effect, easing tension and cares.

In front of the fire, on a platform, stood a memorial made of wood. A ring of eagle feathers laced with gold and precious stones topped the stand. In the middle of the shoulder-high shrine, a nest-like cradle held the healing-stone. The size of a cantaloupe, it purred gently and glowed with a soft, turquoise light as it had done for thousands of years.

Bending Tree motioned to the woman keeping watch and tending the fire. She scurried off to the far corner, retrieving two bowls, one filled with dried venison and berries, and the other with hot tea made with pine needles and sage sweetened with honey.

The two visitors grabbed the food and stuffed their mouths; their hunger was the only real truth that had been uttered. In Erikson's mind, the natives were only useful for the food and information they possessed. Outside of that, they would be considered in the way—an obstacle to be removed like dirt from gold.

Once they noticed the stone, the men slowed their eating to gawk. "Now what be this thing of interest?" Erikson pointed with his greasy chin. "Be it alive, methinks?" He reached a cold hand to the nest, feeling the warmth it generated.

Toby's gaze darted back and forth while he stuffed his mouth.

"This is what interprets our language for us. It is a healing-stone," Bending Tree said.

"*Bliiimey* ..." Erikson whispered to himself. "Could it be?"

Toby mimicked the captain, "*Bliiimey* ..."

"It is the stone that heals," the Chief added.

"*Heeeals* ..." Toby stared holes into the oracle.

"It is the stone of peace."

"*Peeeace* ..." Toby bounced on his frozen toes like a child waiting for his gift.

"The stone knows and understands. It counsels and gives life to us. It is a gift from the mountain for those with an honest heart."

The sight of the stone stirred greed in the captain's heart. He could hardly contain himself, he'd found what others only dreamed of. Erikson resisted the urge to snatch it and run.

"Where's in the world ya find such treasure?" Erikson half asked, half demanded. "Be there any more, me wonders?" He would have tried to read the chief's face, but the stone kept his attention.

"Yes," Bending Tree said. "Skye told of caves in the mountain that are lined with these healing-stones."

Skye? Erikson pondered the name. It meant something to him.

"Skye also said he cannot go back to find more."

"Why's on earth not?" the captain asked.

"No one can. The entrance is lost. Only the mountain knows its location."

Bending Tree gave the history of the stone and told the legend of the fair-skinned man who would deliver it. He also told the incredible story of Skye floating in a giant bubble and about the two healing-stones from the mountain that saved not only the chief's life, but Skye's as well.

"Where be this grand hero now?" Erikson tried to flatter, knowing if he found Skye it would lead to more than the location of the hidden stone. "Surely the good man be not a secret, now be he? It would be mighty nice if'n we be visitin' an honor someone of our own kind. Ya know, someone who be safe and sane fer a change, if'n ya get me drift?"

Bending Tree nodded. "Skye lives on the other side of the mountain with his wife and child. He comes and visits us from time to time. He is a good man, full of compassion."

"Toby," Erikson whispered out the side of his mouth,

"ya can start blessin' the king; I believes we be gettin' the fount'n-o-youth."

"What is this 'fountain of youth' you speak of?" Bending Tree asked.

"The fount'n-o-youth?" Erikson took a step back. With a flick of his eye, he looked the chief over in disbelief. "Can't be tellin' me ya never heard o' the very thing whatcha gots here?"

Bending Tree shrugged. "What is important about children playing in falling water?"

Erikson coughed out a laugh and swatted Toby's back. "Children playin' in water!" He laughed harder. "That be the fount'n-o-youth, Toby."

Toby inhaled a mule-like laugh.

The chief and the woman looked to each other for an answer, but had none.

"The fount'n-o-youth ain't no children playin' in water, Chief," Erikson sputtered out between breaths of laughter. "It be the very thing bringin' our health an' youth back to us, forever. Now, back home we's all thought it be a warm swirlin' pool of magic waters, hidden someplace in this here world of yers, ta dip yeself into an' come out young an' healthy like. But looks like we's all wrong about that one. Who'd ever think it be an oversized egg-shaped rock. An' you's gots one right here o' yer very own. Now, if'n ya wants ta play in water like children do, well, I'm a bettin' thadda be as good a thing ta do as any, if'n ya wants. Be me guest."

The chief's brows lifted. "Yes, I understand. The stone not only healed me of my wounds but made me strong again." He thumped his fist to his chest.

Erikson's large grin faded to a curious smirk, and he narrowed an eye. "Jus' how old ya be now, mate, if'n ya don't mind me askin', that is."

"I have lived eighty-eight winters."

"Eighty-eight winters? Eighty ... eight?" The captain looked at Toby in astonishment, and said before Toby could: "Bless the king!"

It didn't take long for the men to offer to trade their horse and mule for the stone, but the chief said the stone must not leave or be used. It was a symbol of a promise between them and the mountain.

"This gift represents peace, harmony, and health," the chief said. "It is remembering these that make us one with the mountain."

With slick words the men tried tricking him for the location of the other stones, but Bending Tree gave none. "Only Misty knows."

The two visitors ate their fill, warmed themselves, and soon grew tired of these cat-and-mouse games. Erikson became indignant, pointing his long, bony finger at the chief as if he were a subordinate on his ship. "*Mate*," he said, his face skewed in anger, "I's been around thieves an' liars long enough ta know when they ain't tellin' no truth. An' you, matey, be a liar! If'n ya won't tell us good folk here where the bloody cave's hidden or give us this here stone'o yours so's poor people, others than you, can be blessed by its virtue, then maybe someday someone be takin' this here stone from yer greedy little paws." He looked straight into the chief's eyes. "Ain't that right, Toby?"

Toby cowered by Erikson's side, fiddled with his pistol, and nodded. "Aye, Cap."

Erikson turned briskly and stormed from the hut with Toby trailing close behind. Through the waiting crowd they plunged with their hands waving and insults flying. In the excitement of their retreat, Toby took the pistol from his belt and waved it high in the air as he ran to his mule.

Erikson had just reached his horse when Toby squeezed the trigger. The blast shook the nearby snow from the trees; crows and other snowbirds scattered. The sudden percussion scared the mountain people and also took Erikson by surprise. After settling his horse, the captain yanked the pistol from Toby's grip, following it up with a slippery kick to his posterior and a few unsettling words.

The villagers watched the men mount their beasts and trot off through the snow-drifted forest. Bending Tree shook his head. His first instincts had been proven right.

Men with bad hearts—they blame others for what they, themselves are: Liars.

Chapter 10

Fire on the Mountain

"I need more sapphires!"

"What about rubies?" Igneous' eyes glowed with excitement. "You know how good rubies look on you. You want rubies too, don't you?"

"Yes, I'll take some rubies. Emeralds as well, but I must have more sapphires—as many as you can carry. Quickly—they're getting too close."

Igneous knew as well as Misty that if they waited much longer the invasion of treasure seekers would take deeper root and grow stronger. Each day the greater numbers made it harder for them to be uprooted without causing considerable damage to the whole area. Igneous helped prepare their defense.

"Diamonds." Igneous' eyes lit up. "How about diamonds? The way diamonds capture your light is absolutely amazing. You have to have some diamonds— at least one. I can get diamonds, if you want."

"No, no diamonds! They're way too hard to digest.

They'll never do at this late notice. Just make sure you bring more sapphires. Lots more."

Igneous turned and rolled through the gem-coated caverns, humming contentedly to himself and adding an occasional whistle. He stopped first in the sapphire room and rolled to the center.

"All in good time, my child," he whispered, patting the warm surface of Hope. She always seemed to swell and brighten whenever he entered her room. "All in good time and you shall be set free. Chains will again be broken because of you, you'll see—all in good time." It was a litany Igneous always recited for Hope whenever he came anywhere close to her room.

Igneous pulled sapphires from the walls and ceiling as if plucking fruit from a tree. His left arm cradled the glimmering mound of gems like a baby until he'd piled them sufficiently high.

He weaved his way along the glimmering halls, gathering a few handfuls of rubies and emeralds and two diamonds—just in case—then headed back, stopping now and then to retrieve jewels that fell from his grip.

At the edge of the magma pit, where Misty's eye mirrored on the surface, a stack of living-stones towered on the crystal floor of the room. They purred soothingly as they glowed, patiently waiting for Igneous to return.

"I'm back," Igneous announced in a singsong tone. "Where do you want me to put them?"

Misty's eye blinked and turned to him. "Next to the living stones, of course. I believe you know what to do next."

"That I do, my frothy friend. That I do." Igneous picked a stone from the middle of the pile, causing several to cascade down from where he pulled it. "Just like old times, you and me, huh?" He stroked the stone casually before breaking it in two against his side. The stone's hypnotic song ended and the scent of its elixir thickened the air.

"Mixin' and brewin' …"

He dropped a handful of sapphires, two rubies, and a single emerald into its shell.

"… and stirrin' and swirlin' …"

He closed the two halves together and shook them with vigor, almost violently.

"… and whippin' and bubblin'."

He opened the shell and dumped its lumpy contents into the magma below. Instantly, streams of hot gas blew high into the cavity of Misty's mouth, dragging multiple colors of liquid in their wake. Igneous paused for a moment to watch, wide eyed, as if it were a display of fireworks. He took a satisfied breath. "Ahh, it feels good to be cooking again!"

He threw the two empty shells into the pit. When they hit the surface of the magma, they spun in twisted circles, sizzling and skipping over the ripples of the hot pool until they eventually disintegrated into a puff of turquoise smoke.

Misty's eye narrowed. "Igneous, you know I don't like it when I can't see. I must always know what's going on."

"Oops, sorry about that. Sometimes it's hard to resist the 'dance of the shell.' It doesn't happen too often, and from where I'm at it's amazing to watch. But I'll try to contain myself—promise."

"Let's hope so. Now please, can we get back to our work? It's going to take some time to get prepared. And if you could shake the sapphires a bit longer it would help in digesting the formula. It takes less energy from me and I've been feeling a little out of sorts."

Igneous continued to break, shake, pour, and watch the contents of the stones flash before his childlike eyes. Around him, the discarded shells lay scattered at his feet. He had one more to go before his part was finished. After cracking the last stone, and peeking to see if Misty was watching, he slipped one of the diamonds in with the rest of the gems. A satisfied smile crossed his face as he shook it more vigorously than before.

"Almost done here. Only one more and she's all yours."

"One more?" Misty sounded queasy. "I'm not sure if I can take another."

"Sure you can. There's always room for one more. You can do it."

Misty sighed. "I'll try. But don't blame me if I can't keep it down."

Igneous felt ecstatic, and shook the stone again for good measure before easing himself to the edge of the pit. His breathing became more rapid, and a sly grin slid onto his face. "Yep, almost done." He pulled the shell apart. "The last one and she's *aaall* yours."

Slowly, he drained the thick elixir into the bubbling soup. "Here she comes."

A radiant flash burst before him like all the others and, as before, Igneous watched with enthusiasm. "Not going to be long now." He could hardly contain himself. "The last of the—"

The most awful gurgling sound suddenly belched from below. Misty's eye faded into a tight squint and disappeared in the depths.

Igneous held his nose and his eyes grew big with anticipation. A hollow spot abruptly caved in, in the middle of the churning broth, and waves of color bubbled to the surface. It looked like a catastrophic storm swirling in a whirlpool of magma. Then, with one gigantic burp, a slimy, white object shot out at an incredible speed. It hit the side of Misty's inner mouth, ricocheted past Igneous and into a tunnel opening, where it lodged itself in the back wall, knocking a good many crystals to the cobbled floor.

Misty's eye came back strong and fuming.

"I can fix that!" Igneous pointed behind him at the damaged wall.

"What in the world were you thinking? I told you no diamonds! I almost lost the whole thing before I was ready."

"Ah, but you didn't, did you?" Igneous leaned over with a smile, and surveyed the angry eye. "Feeling better now? Come on, tell me how you feel? Better, don't you?"

Misty's eye relaxed and looked around as if thinking. "Yes, for that matter, everything is settling much better. How did you know? No … You shouldn't have taken it upon yourself without warning me, especially after I said 'no diamonds'."

"Now, now, I know how you get when consuming large quantities of sapphires; indigestion hits you right between the fault and a hard spot. I'm happy to see you didn't need another diamond."

Igneous held up the other gem pinched between his stony fingers. "Guess I'll have to put this one back, hmm? Unless, of course …"

"Oh no, you can put that back where you found it. One was sufficient, thank you."

"You're welcome." Igneous grinned impishly.

He turned and headed back down the corridor then turned back with an added thought. "One more thing I've got to do before I go, I promise."

Before Misty could object, a shower of shells tumbled down to him.

"What does it mean?"

The sun dimmed behind the western slope of the mountain and cold stars sparkled on a blanket of black. Misty's ghostly mouth glowed in the dusk where flashes of colored light sparked above its rim.

"Misty knows of the foreigners," Bending Tree said to Yenene while watching the mountain. "I believe he is making ready a war of his own. It concerns him as it does us."

Yenene pulled his bearskin blanket tighter around his shoulders. "It would explain his tears of anger. The timing would be right. Many men are gathering below, digging the earth, and warring with each other. It angers me as well."

"Yes, it is disturbing to wonder what may become of our home, our way of life, and how it could change us all."

Yenene was upset. "We must never change. If Misty fights, we will fight! We will protect our way and all that Misty has given, even unto death. This is our home, my Chief. They must leave."

The Chief turned to his friend. He drew a long breath, and white vapor floated away in the bitter air. "That, my friend, is something we have never done—fight. The act itself would be 'change,' would it not? A change that would certainly alter us forever, but not necessarily for the better."

Bending Tree turned his gaze back to the night sky and watched the colored sparks grow in number and height. His brow creased in thought. Misty was building momentum. "No, there will be no blood on our hands unless it is forced. Then it will be I who will gladly make the first change. There is always a time to consider change, for sometimes it is good. But you are right, Yenene, our ways must always be with the mountain. That can never change."

Yenene's mind was as stiff as his fingers in the cold. He stared at the frozen ground and shoved some snow with his foot. "What, then, are we to do?"

"Look." Bending Tree pointed to the mountain. "Misty is already doing. We will wait. And we will be ready—to make a change."

The two stood in silence, watching the mountain's wrath build. It gave a sudden surge and the earth quaked. The men braced each other but the quakes knocked them to the frozen ground.

Up from the belly of the mountain and out of its jagged mouth, a streaming fountain of colored cinders burst forth, blasting the dark into day. The flaming jewels sizzled through the chilled air all the way to their targets. Snow melted around them.

Embers streaked like meteors and snapped like pitch-laden logs roasting on a grate. The fiery gems soared as if with purpose as though each had a target in mind.

Emeralds, rubies, and a multitude of blazing sapphires pelted the mountain's slope, smote the forest, and bounced through the trees where the foreigners froze helplessly. The avalanche of flames tumbled their way toward a hundred camps on Misty's slopes, never once touching the trees or threatening the village.

The flaming jewels ignited the invaders' shelters. Gold melted back to the earth, and their beasts scattered about the snow-drifted forest. Ironically, men caught on fire from the very thing their souls were on fire to possess.

In the distance, at the foot of Misty, the lone, silver-clad figure stood on a pinnacle of rock, observing the dramatic display of flaming stones. The showering brilliance reflected in its silver eyes, and it wanted to learn more.

A song sprang forth from its silver tongue. Tearfully beautiful at first, it morphed into perverted, diminished tones, muffled by blasts from the mountain. It raised its arms above its hooded head—polished, gem-laced hands reached for the display, as if trying to grab what it could not have.

From the straining fingertips, sparks drizzled and floated harmlessly to the ground. Again the fingers labored, but produced only a dismal trickle of sparks. The creature stopped to study the mountain, and then, raising its voice, sang a song more intense and lewd than before. The magnificently-crafted arms and hands shot into the air, fingers curling with intensity. This time sparks sprang forth in a silver shower and gained force with each moment.

The creature, now understanding the mechanics of its flow, relaxed in its creating, enjoying the thrill. But still it wanted more.

Slowly, its fingers straightened, and the creature siphoned streams of colored, electric waves from each of the precious stones adorning its body. In a sudden flash, sparks shot higher into the air until the creature was lost in the shower of its own geyser. Its song, now dancing hideously with the rhythmic beat of its heart, commanded the shower to change to any color it chose. For several minutes the creature played with its counterfeit creation, then, satisfied, it extinguished its light and disappeared into the smoky shadows.

Chapter 11
The Power of Greed

The night lasted long in its winter chill, and the dawn arrived gray under a smoke-filled sky. Morning revealed a sad multitude of shivering, soot-stained men wandering about burned camps. They had come to the mountain seeking riches but now scavenged for survival, and pillaged and fought for each other's gear.

Far away, Bending Tree watched the people in distress and shook his head. In spite of his desire to see them gone from the mountain, he must help simply because he saw people in need.

"Honovi. Takota. Tamarack." Bending Tree called through the woods. "Come."

The three young men trotted in, kicking up crusty snow, while Bending Tree watched the forest slope below. Snow and ice crystals hung on one side of the pine trees while the side that faced the heat of Misty's fury looked dry as summer.

Honovi arrived first. "Is something wrong, my Chief?"

Bending Tree waited for the other young men before speaking. "We are needed," he said. "Men will die if we do not help."

"Men?" Tamarack asked. "Surely you do not speak of the foreigners?"

"Yes," the chief said. "Food must be gathered—blankets and skins—as much as we can afford from our supplies."

Honovi grunted. "We should not help men who wound our land … who threaten our people and our way of life."

"I agree," Tamarack said. "If they die, they die. It is Misty's will that they be punished."

Bending Tree took a deep breath of cold air and turned it into a warm puff of steam. "Punished, perhaps, but if Misty wanted them dead he would do so; instead he chose to destroy their camps. He is slow to anger and swift with compassion, as I am with you right now." The chief's face had a look to it that would make anyone's stomachs knot up. "Show compassion, my young braves, and in your time of need, compassion will shine on you."

Takota directed his eyes to the ground in thought before settling them back on his leader. "My Chief, if we do not help these men in their need, will they seek us out and war with us as they do with each other?"

Tamarack saw the logic. "They will come to our village looking for help like the two strangers before."

Bending Tree's brow arched inquisitively. "You do not like this then?"

Honovi shook his head. "The ways of the strangers are not good. If they stay, we are all in danger."

"Then what are we to do?" Already knowing the answer, Bending Tree encouraged their input.

"To assure their safety is to assure ours as well,"

Honovi concluded.

Takota stepped forward. "It would be wise if we were to go below, away from our people, and help them there."

Tamarack had the same idea. "We will find their horses and return them. Then we will lead them back down the mountain and set them safely on their way home."

Bending Tree nodded proudly. His aged eyes glistened in the cold air. "Then do as you have wisely advised, my braves. Take more men with you and distribute what we can spare. Go now. They are in great need."

The morning passed slowly with the dispensing of goods. Most of the victims were grateful, some skeptical, a few were too proud to accept, and some wanted more than what was offered. Overall, it went well until one of the village men approached a particular campsite.

Two men lay waiting, shivering behind a patch of oak brush. "Well now, mate," whispered a voice, "would ya look-a that savage parading his bloody goods in front o' our noses like that."

"What's he teasin' us fer, Cap?" Toby whined.

"Indeed, me Toby, what fer? A wee bit rude, wouldn't ya say?"

"Aye, bloody rude!" Toby's lower lip protruded in a pout as he watched from under the hood of his bushy brows.

"Well now," the captain said and placed a reassuring arm around Toby, "would it be pleasin' ya then if'n the selfish savage be harpooned … eh?"

"Thatta teach 'em, fer sure." A grin of satisfaction raised his stubbled cheeks.

"That settles it then, Toby, me lad." Erikson patted the thick shoulder with a skinny hand. "We best be takin' what's ours."

Toby's eyes widened. "Then we can divvy up stuff between us, likes we use ta, an' sell what's we don't need to all them stupids—bless da king."

"Aye, me lardy 'king blesser,' an' get us the bloody 'ell out o' here an' over to the other side before anyone catches wind o' the renegade with the secret." Erikson's voice grew hard. "Now, fetch me musket."

Toby ran, crunching through the snow to the captain's horse, pulled out a long-barreled musket from a mule skin sheath, and ran back. It had already been loaded with gunpowder packed behind a single lead slug. Toby slipped, and the gun flailed in his hand as he tried to regain his footing before falling smack on his backside.

Erikson knew well Toby's trigger-happy fingers and disliked the way the gun waved his way. He tromped quickly to Toby's side and, with a few curses, snatched the musket with one hand and planted a foot on Toby's shoulder to break his hold. The captain scrambled back to the oak brush, put a knee to the frozen earth, took a calming breath, and aimed the musket.

The gun fired and a cry fell muffled in the thick forest. In red snow, an Anasazi man in the prime of his life lay murdered.

They ran to their fallen prey and took turns kicking him, rejoicing in the goods and horse they had just claimed. Toby threw things about while the captain dictated what to keep for themselves. The rest they planned to sell to other crippled camps for top dollar. When they finished their business, their quest would lead them to the other side of the mountain, a three-day race, in search of the location to the greatest prize of all: the secret caves of the healing stones.

"Hurry up with the horse, ya bloody little hairball."

"Aye, Cap. Ain't gonna be but a few shakes 'ere with da saddle an' we's be on our way."

"Be makin' it snappy then. We got's ta get there before the others catch wind o' the stone. Now hurry it up!"

The lanky captain took a few steps forward and stared out over the frozen land. His gaze matched the weather—cold. Behind the narrow slits of eyes, his mind wandered in dark places while he whispered his thoughts.

"Pickin's gonna be easy with the renegade. He knows the location all right, or I be beatin' it out o' him, if'n I have ta." He smiled at the thought. "Easy prey ... aye, easy. Then I be dealin' with her, the ungrateful snip. And no one's gonna knows but me. Jus' me ... me ... me ... bless the—" He ran a thin hand across his face and sighed in exasperation. "Blimey, if'n he ain't got's me blessin' royalty too, the bloody little ... *Toobyyy!*"

Outside, Skye tended his horse while Pearl and the baby were inside minding the house. From the sunlit window, Pearl saw Skye stroking the horse's neck as it ate the hay he'd harvested during summer. The crisp afternoon air caused their breath to steam around their heads while the snow sparkled like diamonds in the sun. She smiled and cradled the sleeping child close, feeling content in the warmth of her home. Then she saw Skye wave to some unseen visitors.

Wonderful, company from the village would be nice.

In her mind she made plans for dinner.

But these were not the native people she expected. Two men cloaked in blankets rode double on a tired horse, leading a pack-mule loaded with blankets, food, and a bundle of sticks.

What brings them all this way in this weather? she wondered.

There was an exchange of greetings before the taller of the two men stiffly dismounted. The shorter, stocky man slid from behind the saddle and fell, slipping to the ground. He struggled back to his oversized feet and brushed snow from his coat.

Pearl chuckled as she watched, until the tall man reached a thin arm over the short man's balding head and jabbed a finger into her husband's shoulder. Tempers escalated, voices rose, and Skye demanded them to leave.

Above the heated talk, Pearl thought she heard the word 'stowaway.' She drew in a startled breath; she recognized the voice. She thrust a deerskin coat over her arms and swaddled her baby securely in rabbit fur. With the child to her chest, she opened the door.

Dear Misty, what do they want with us?

The door closing behind her reminded Pearl of a guillotine making its final drop.

High in the air, an eagle circled around the box-of-dead-trees—the name the giant birds gave the cabin. She watched three men on the ground pushing, punching, and shouting. The stocky man fell to the snow several times before grabbing the heels of the blond man. As the blond man tried to escape the clutch of brawny hands, his foot connected with the stocky man's face. Blood sprayed everywhere.

The eagle saw that the blond man fought well and her heart cheered for him; it pleased her to see him holding his own. Then a long, sharp object flickered in the thin man's hand and a cry reached her ears as the blond man's body fell limp in a pool of red.

A woman screamed and ran into the woods. One of the men pointed to her, a shout erupted, and they scuttled after her. The woman ran through deep snow over a small hill behind the cabin, eventually reaching a frozen creek where she rested near an oak bush.

The eagle's heart beat wildly with fear for the woman as she dug a hole in the snow under a bush and placed a bundle there before running again.

Before long the thin man caught the woman. They struggled; he shook her violently by the shoulders and slapped her so hard she fell to the snow.

The shorter man yanked her up and held her from behind while the thin man held the sharp metal object once more before using it. Her screams sent chills through the eagle.

Misty shook. Rocks split and the earth opened in a multitude of strategic spots, spewing fire and gas. The two men ran without direction and only just managed to dodge the fire and fissures that opened before them, but not without the mountain singeing their clothes, hair, and a bit of their tainted souls.

The eagle clan knew Misty to be slow with anger, but the senseless murder of the Anasazi man engaged in a mission of mercy, and now the slaughter of the man and woman, made the mountain furious. Murder didn't exist in the history of the tribe, nor had the mountain ever taken a life before. Both mountain and tribe would be scarred forever.

The lower slopes of the mountain had the eerie look of a disaster. Large patches of snow dissolved around cracks in the earth where smoke squeezed from the fissures, lingering close to the ground. Shrubs smoldered and sparks drifted in the cold breeze. It seemed justice had been served, but it left a lingering bitter taste.

The eagle watched as steamy tears fell from Misty's mountaintop and turned into a turquoise cloud that wrapped both the village and the box-of-dead-trees like an eagle's wing around her young. The intrusions were over for now, but the scars would remain as a reminder.

The sun lowered its blood-red face on the horizon, sending shadows stabbing across the mountain—anxious, it seemed, for this morbid day to end.

Chapter 12
The Orphan

A tiny chunk of snow rolled down a small embankment and skipped across a frozen stream. Soon another one followed with several more trailing behind, spinning lazily on the ice. The movement caught a crow's attention. It fluttered to the frozen stream where it stopped by one of the spinning chips of snow and tipped its head sideways, observing the object. It cackled at it, and then with its beak, shattered the hardened cake into ice crystals. Another chip spun, bouncing off its foot. The crow jumped into the air, cawing in surprise.

The noise and movement of the bird summoned the other crows scouring the area for any remains of the dead. They found bloodstained snow nearby and knew something close must be hurt or dying—their meal wasn't too far off.

On the knoll of the embankment where oak brush grew in thick groves, the snow bulged then fell from a spot under the branches. Chips of snow dislodged with each movement, skipping down the crusted slope to the icy stream below.

One by one, the black scavengers dropped to the frozen water, *cawing* their excitement. Their twitching heads twisted this way and that in their search for an easy meal. In greater numbers they dropped from the sky, adding to the confusion on the ground. Some rebounded in the air a few feet, searching for the fallen prey then floated back down. Soon the white ground was freckled with black objects moving up and down as if they were kneading snow into bread. The drifting scent of blood added to the frenzy. If anything remained to be found, they would find it before night could swallow sight of their dinner.

In the distance, the eagle soared mechanically in figure-eight patterns above Misty's western rim. Her keen eyes veered down to the knotted slope of thick pine and rock, and found the sad, empty home.

Just up from an open field of snow by the cabin, the sight of crows fussing over an object annoyed the eagle. They pulled it. They dragged it. They poked at it. They even managed to lift it from the ground and drop it. They surrounded the object and pounced upon it, obscuring it in a flurry of beating wings. Agitated, but curious, the eagle kept her eyes fixed on the scene below.

"Dumb scavengers, always pecking at something filthy," she sneered. Her feelings were in turmoil and, in spite of the distance, she didn't appreciate the commotion. Her mind filled with disturbing thoughts— thoughts that would drive her crazy if she didn't settle them.

"Why didn't I help?" she scolded herself aloud, beating her wings faster and faster, still flying in figure-eight patterns.

The violent murder of the man and the woman

appalled her. It was within her ability to help, but she did nothing. The mountain eagles, in general, were uninterested in the affairs of other animals—especially man. They were usually content to keep their distance and observe from far away. But this particular eagle's emotions were different—always had been.

"Why didn't I?" she scolded herself again, still ripping angry figure-eights through the air.

She often perched on a boulder overlooking the box-of-dead-trees, fascinated at how the humans cared for each other and how the baby brought happiness to their life. She wanted that kind of life. In her own way she lived vicariously through the human family, but always from a distance.

"Why all the dumb rules to stay away from man anyway? They've done nothing to us."

It was hard sorting out her feelings, so she flew the mindless infinity patterns while she tried to deal with her emotions. Again her attention diverted to the crows, still tumbling about in their frenzy. She became more perturbed. "They're not there, you stupid crows!" she screamed at them, knowing they couldn't hear from this distance, but feeling it would release some built-up pressure.

Why were the dumb birds making such a racket anyway? Didn't they see the ground swallow the people up? A tear puddled at the corner of her eye. "There is no food."

She remembered the horror as Misty had opened the earth in many places, like jaws snapping at their prey, and shot showering sparks of fire at the killers. When all had become quiet again, she saw the earth open beneath the two dead humans, as Misty took them into his care— a proper burial.

"They're gone, and they're never coming back." Tears puddled her eyes, and a shaking breath choked up against the pain that burned in her heart. "It was I ... I who let them die. The father ..." she recounted to herself, banking a fast, tight corner. "The mother ..." She turned her body hard in the other direction and pushed with her twenty-foot wing span in the opposite direction. "The chil—" A sudden shock went up her spine, and she faltered in the sky. *The child—where is the child?*

She remembered the woman burying something under a bush close to the stream, right about where the ... Then she heard it, mixed with the crows' chatter—a faint cry.

"The child!" Rage surged through her as she identified with the deceased woman's desperation to save her baby. Her full ire focused on the flock of scavenger birds. The birds continued to pull and prod at the bundle, methodically ripping at it with hungry beaks.

"The child, dear Misty, they've found the child."

She banked hard into the smoky wisps that lingered in the air, flapped several powerful strokes, and then tucked her wings tight for a fast free-fall. Her eyes narrowed to dark slits. She zeroed in on the flock and screeched a horrifying scream.

In seconds, she had reached her destination and plowed a satisfying, thick line through the center of the dark squall with her outstretched talons. Black feathers rained like ashes to the frozen earth. Dozens of scavengers lay dead or mortally wounded, and the remaining flock scattered in flight, cackling as they left behind one angry eagle.

The eagle glided around, sounding out a warning to the departing birds, before she landed beside the dark, frayed object. The blast of her wings blew the snowy ground into a white cloud against the setting sun. A shrill cry met her from the bundle at her feet. Breath after breath, the child convulsed with terrifying screams until its throat became raw and weak.

The eagle's heart broke at the sound of innocence mistreated. She drew the child closer, intuitively cooing a warm reply. For a moment, the crying subsided to a whine.

She turned her head sideways to observe the tattered package. Past a spot pecked open by the crows, she saw red scratches that leaked onto its body. The bundle moved and a soft cry reached her ears. Cautiously, she leaned her head down, tugged at the bundle with her beak, and revealed a baby human. The baby's head and ear bled in several spots from beak scratches, and its tiny lips shivered. Its blue eyes met the yellow eyes of the eagle, and the infant's whimpering eased.

"You're coming with me," the eagle cooed. She folded the tattered rabbit skin back over the baby's head, and a tear squeezed from her eye and slid down her beak.

She wrapped a clawed foot around the bundle, stood her full height of over six feet, and looked sharply around—defying any danger. Steam blew from her nostrils. She found no threat ... only the fragmented bodies of greedy birds strewn in a sea of black feathers. Satisfied, she closed her talons around the child, spread her wings, and lifted into the icy air with a single push.

Long, even strokes pushed the eagle with her trophy up to the mountain's summit and over the spot where the child's father had first laid eyes on Elysium Valley last spring. The eagle shot out above the hidden valley, breaching the layer of lingering smoke, and sailed like an arrow over the lake. Winter seemed to have little effect on this part of the mountain; the water never froze, but remained at a constant warm temperature.

Two eagles approached from the towering cliffs near Elysium Lake. She turned up her beak and tightened her grip on her passenger. The eagles soon circled her flanks.

"Hey, Windy, what you got there, a rabbit?"

"None of your business," she snapped. "Go away and be curious someplace else." Windy drew the bundle closer to her body.

"Ah, come on, Windy, you're gonna share some with us, aren't you?"

Windy gave a sharp, appalled look. "Not on your life! Go away, Trekker, and take your oversized friend with you."

Trekker continued to probe. "Hey ..." He glanced at Thunderwing. "... let's say you and I have a little peek at what kind of game Windy's got there?"

"I'm game if you're game." Thunder made a teasing attempt at the bundle.

Windy shrieked and swerved from his reach. The sudden jerk made the child cry. "Now look what you've done." She scowled.

The two eagles looked at each other in horror.

"Whoa now, Windy," Thunderwing said. "You don't have a man-child there, do ya?"

"Yeah," Trekker added, "you're not gonna—"

"I am not! How dare you think such a thing, particularly about one of us eagles, let alone about me? Now you stay away and let us be, you hear?"

"Now, now," Trekker said, "you know it's impossible for us to hide anything from any of us, unless, of course, any of us aren't actually looking. It can't be done."

Thunderwing rolled his eyes. "What Trekker thinks he's saying, is that you know very well that we eagles are honest and can't easily lie or keep anything hidden. Our eyes are sharp enough to see right through the slightest guilt on any beak."

"Yeah," Trekker said, "seeing is believing, and we seeee everything. So what do ya say you let us seeee what only you have seeeen, but don't want anyone else to seeee."

"Yeah, Windy, Trekker's right. There's no escaping us, you seeee?"

Windy gave a sideways glance at the two, a look of defeat on her face. "Yes, I *SEE* what you mean. All right, all right. If you want to know, you'll have to go gather the rest of us over to my nest so I can tell everyone at the same time. I don't want to have to repeat this." Her irritated look turned into a scowl. "Well, don't just glide there with your beaks gaping; you look as dumb as crows. *Go!*"

The two adolescent eagles gave each other sidelong glances of excitement.

"Hey," Trekker said to Thunder, "this may be as fun as that strange bubble we chased to the village last summer."

"No way, nothing could be as fun as that."

The two cousins banked away, flapping their wings and chattering in excitement—breaking news needed to be told.

Glad to be rid of the two, Windy continued the flight to her nest. When the cliffs approached, she turned her wings and flapped them gently until she rested in the center of her knitted home of twigs and feathers. She released the bundle and proceeded to remove the rabbit fur from the shivering man-child. With one claw hooked on the skin, she used her beak to tug at the leather strings that bound it.

A wave of relief washed over her—*a girl*. It couldn't have been better for Windy. "From what I've seen, little one, girls are less of a wingfull than boys," she said, rubbing the baby's belly playfully with her beak. She paused a moment, unable to keep her eyes off the child. "But something tells me it's not going to be as easy as all that with you."

It eased her mind seeing that the scratches left by the crows were superficial. She cooed a melody of sorts and spread the skins over the nest for a softer cushion against the rough wooden sticks. Then, doing what mother eagles do, she plucked softer feathers from her sides and belly and covered the rabbit skin. Finally, she positioned herself over the baby and rested her warm underbelly on top. Her wings cupped around the infant, and blocked out all wind and cold. With the heat she generated, it didn't take long for the baby to stop shivering. She felt the infant snuggle deep into her eagle-down and experienced for the first time the joy of motherhood.

The redness from the child's cheeks, and the blue from her lips, faded nicely, but the girl still whimpered. Windy tried to comfort her, but nothing seemed to help. She checked the sticks, but none poked against the child, and plenty of warm air circulated beneath the eagle for the baby to breathe. What could it be? "Ah, but of course." A worried look came over her face. "Oh my, little one, what do baby humans eat? Could it be worms and other bugs you want? Maybe a mouse or a squirrel is more to your liking. Let's see. I've seen the mountain people planting gardens and picking from their crops. Could that be something you'll eat?"

Think, she ordered herself. "How will I ever know? Whatever it is, I've got to find out fast or you'll suck those little fingers right off your pretty little hand."

She marveled at the tiny fingers working in and out, and leaned in closer. The baby reached up and grabbed the pointed end of her beak. Windy giggled, and looked cross-eyed down at her. "My, what an eagle couldn't do with workable wings like those."

In the distance, eagle cries rang off the cliffs. A good dozen of her kin sailed closer. The last of the sun glittered off their golden feathers before it disappeared below the western rim, leaving the sky brushed with streaks of orange.

Windy gave a series of calls to let them know that visitors were welcome. One by one they came, until they'd filled the ledges around her nest.

When all were present and attentive, she spoke. "As you know, I am no longer a fledgling nor am I an old hen." She looked at each one individually. "You also know that, for some reason, my eggs have never been able to hatch. Many were lost and I have always been without a chick to mother. I've often wondered why. Years ago, I asked Misty why everything is so perfect here and no one lacks anything, but still I have no chick of my own.

"Today, there has been much trouble on the mountain. Foreign people came to dig for something. They harmed each other and they harmed Misty's land. The mountain people have lost a man because of them and the family who lived in the box-of-dead-trees on the other side has also been attacked. They are both dead."

The eagles chattered at the news.

"I know it is sad to hear. I also know some of you believe that I spend too much time looking in on them, getting too close. But the way they lived and the respect they gave Misty and his land made me respect them. I had to look in on them."

She fidgeted over her new addition, not yet used to the life that squirmed there and not ready to reveal her. Then she recounted the tale of what had transpired that day, right up until she had discovered the flock of birds.

This wasn't the time for Windy to challenge the traditions of the eagles, so she took a deep breath before continuing.

"A flock of crows found their infant hidden in the snow and attacked it. This time I couldn't stand by and watch another slaughter. Forgive me," she begged, "I couldn't let it die."

Slowly, she lifted herself and folded one of her wings back.

Chapter 13
Surprise Adoption

"Good heavens. That's a man-child!"

"A man-child?"

"This is not good, not good at all."

"Oh, I think it's wonderful."

"What will you do with this … this … ?"

"You will keep her, won't you, darling?"

"Yes, yes, that's what we'd like to know."

"Now, ladies, it's none of our business."

"But it's not one of us."

"Shouldn't matter, should it?"

"No, put it back where you found it. If it was meant to die, it was meant to die."

"No, we must take it to the man village."

"Good idea. They'll know what to do with it."

"Yes, their chief will know what to do. Take it to him."

"All agreed?"

"No, no, no!"

A sudden scream pierced the air and stopped the

conversation. Windy lowered herself back down over the crying infant and raised her voice to the others. "My dear eagles, do be quiet. Stop bickering and let me speak before the sun's light goes out."

They unruffled their feathers and tucked their wings back to their sides, giving each other curious looks.

"Before I say anything else," Windy continued, "I must first tell you this. This child is hungry. I don't suspect she's eaten anything since early this morning."

She scanned the eagles and found the two she wanted. "Trekker and Thunder, you were both so eager to poke your beaks into my business that I insist you become partial guardians to this child. Your first duty is to go at once and catch a rabbit, and not any of those scrawny ones with the big eyes and fleas you've been finding down beyond the woods. Bring one back to me. Off with you both before the sun sleeps. Quickly."

Both birds looked perplexed at Windy's command. They'd never seen her so determined.

"Now, boys!"

All eyes shifted to them. The two glanced at each other, not knowing what to say, then in a flurry of feathers, they left.

"I tell you, my dear family," Windy continued, looking each one in the eye. "I've made up my mind. As of right now this child has aunts, uncles, grandparents, a mother, and a home, and I thank you kindly for volunteering."

They all looked as dumbfounded as Trekker and Thunderwing.

"Now, please listen and I will tell you all I know concerning this child. I'll try to be as quick as I can so that you can all get back to your nests and sleep on what I am about to say."

Curious, they stopped fidgeting and gave Windy their attention.

"This may sound crazy, but ever since I learned to fly, I made trips to the forbidden area at the top of Misty. I know our rule, to never to go to that region and disturb the mountain. But as you know, a young eagle's curiosities can sometimes get the better of her. So it was true with me long ago."

"You always were the curious one," her cousin, Stardust, said.

"Yes, too curious for your own good, it seems." Uncle Windstorm was always cynical.

The eldest of the eagle clan, Screaming Eagle, put his foot down. "Stop it, you two, let her finish. I'm sure there's a perfectly good reason for her disobeying our traditions. Windy?"

This might be tougher than I thought. Windy swallowed hard and worked to keep a calm face. "As I was saying, I flew to the ridge top and looked in. Its depths could not be seen from where I stood, so I flew deeper into the mountain, until I saw hot, bubbling liquid filling every space of Misty's mouth. An enormous eye appeared. The eye looked right at me. *'Watch,'* a voice gurgled from the depths. The eye faded into a series of pictures, each one melting into the next."

"What did you see?" Stardust asked.

"What I *saw*," Windy continued, giving Stardust a look, "I kept secret all these years. Now that this child has come to me, I am certain of its meaning. It concerns us all."

"What?" Stardust interrupted. "What does it mean? How does it concern us? Who—?"

"Staaar—I'll tell you, but you've got to stop interrupting. Okay? This is what I saw ..."

Every beak hung open and the group huddled closer, to catch every word.

"A flash of lightning crossed an empty sky and its light splintered into a million other lights. The lights revealed a human arm stretching across the ocean to the shores of our world. Like claws, its fingers dug into the sands and quivered. Black fleas jumped from the hand onto the shore. They hopped about, and made their way, like a plague, through the forests and hills, darkening everything they touched in our world. Also from the hand, jumped two other creatures; these were white. The dark fleas pursued the smaller white creatures, but they eluded the black plague. The white creatures wandered, and found their way to the west side of Misty, and hid there. The two became three then the two turned red and faded away, leaving the one.

"'Behold, your child,' the voice of the mountain said to me, 'take her, keep her, and raise her as one of your own.'

"Again the scene changed. This time it was of Misty in a mood I had never seen before. Colored fire blew a mile into the air. I heard a sound like that of a thousand eagles screaming, then Misty cried. Molten tears showered down in a stream of cinders, burning everything they touched.

"I saw a new eagle emerge from the cinders and take off into the sky. It was white and larger than any of us here. Our queen had finally come.

"Then I saw something I still don't understand. You were flying with her, but nowhere could I see myself. All my life I've been waiting for the one to come. Where was I, and where were you all going with the queen?

"All the images faded away, and the eye reappeared in the lava. It was then that I finally withdrew my gaze. I experienced such sadness that I found myself crying at all I'd seen. Where were you all going without me? I was so alone. Then Misty spoke:

"'Windy, why do you cry? All is not lost, as you might be thinking. Trust goes beyond believing. If you believe, there is always a dream come true. It has been said:

> *'When things turn bad, the bad turn good,*
> *Good turned up the way it should*
> *Evil struck this old earth*
> *Virtue shall come from a fiery birth*
> *Saved by eagles, raised on high*
> *Wings like snow rule Misty's sky*
> *When healing waters touch all men*
> *Then queen she'll be of Misty's land'"*

Windy fell quiet. The eagles didn't know what to say or think. The baby beneath Windy began to cry again. Windy looked up. With tears seeping from her eyes, she spoke her last thought. "I believe this to be the child from the vision, and I will name her Mariah. The making of history is right here in our midst, and it looks like we are all in this together."

Trekker and Thunderwing whisked their way back to Windy's nest, joyfully wailing out a hunter's victory song:

> *"Flying high, a kill to spy,*
> *No more hunts with mud in the eye*
> *We sharpened our beaks, we cleaned our claws,*
> *We'll find a meal to feed our jaws*
> *Hi ho a diddly doe,*
> *Come now, prey, we need your soul*
> *Hi he a diddly dee, food for me and baby."*

On the high note of 'baby,' Thunderwing landed perfectly in front of Windy, sporting a large rabbit. Two seconds later, Trekker barreled in right over the top of him. They both slid to an embarrassing stop, and Trekker clutched something within one of his outstretched talons.

"Geeze, Thunder." Trekker snapped. "Would you quit stopping short like that all the time? You almost made me drop this."

Dazed, Thunderwing gathered his composure while Trekker held out his leg, and proudly displayed his catch. He tried to swallow a laugh. "For you, Windy. A little something I picked up on the way to the lake while Thunder fussed in the woods with those stupid rabbits."

Within his claw, flopping about, lay a pitifully tiny fish. The small gesture dismantled the tension. The eagles burst into cackling laughter. Trekker always had that effect on them.

Soon after, the eagles made ready to leave. The ladies reached out and nuzzled Windy with their beaks.

"We'll be back," some said as they departed. Others nodded proudly. "We believe in you." Only a few said they'd have to sleep on it. But one older eagle, Aunt Cloudcast, couldn't wait another day. "I must see the man-child once more, dearie, quickly now."

Windy felt happy to show her again. In the end, in their own way, they all gave her their blessings. Thunderwing and Trekker ended up being the last to leave.

"I want to thank you boys for helping me out like that," Windy said. "Even if I was a little snappy with you, it means a lot to me, you know?"

"Was nothing, Miss Windy," Thunderwing replied. "Glad to do it. Although I'm a little sore, I might add." He glared at Trekker.

"I couldn't help myself," Trekker said. "You were standing right in the way. And the fish, well, it was too good to pass up. Besides, it looked like all those stuffed feathers hovering over you like crows needed a little unstuffing."

"Well, you did that very well, thank you," replied Windy. "But I'll thank you even more if you go put that baby fish back in the lake where he belongs until he's old enough to actually be a meal. Good night to you, Trekker, I'll see you tomorrow." She gave him a peck on the cheek and turned to Thunderwing. "Will you stay a little while longer? I need your help again."

"Sure, Windy, anything for you."

"Great. This is what I need you to do. Will you please take your rabbit and make long, thin strips of meat from it for me? This baby is going to give me such a headache if I don't do something about her hunger."

Thunderwing did as she asked and made short work of his catch.

"Windy …" he cautioned when he finished, "best you stay clear of the forest, and let me and Trekker get you your food."

The tone in his voice startled Windy and she snuggled the baby closer. "Why, what's wrong with the forest?"

Thunder looked out over the valley as if he were searching for something. "I don't know, it's been a little strange in there lately. Creepy would be more like it."

"Creepy, strange? What's creepy about our forest?"

"It's not so much the forest, as what lurks there. Something sings like a thousand songbirds, but no one's there singing. Something sparkles in dark shadows, then disappears. And something smells of smoke, but there is no fire."

He cleared his throat and turned to look into Windy's

frightened eyes. "Trekker and I saw something a few days ago and went to investigate, but the only thing we found were the remains of animals—all dead, with bloody holes around their hearts. Please, Windy, don't go there. Trekker and I will bring you all you need, okay?"

"Yes, of course." Windy nodded. "Dear Misty, what could it be?"

"We don't know yet, but we're keeping a lookout. In the meantime, don't worry too much. Just stay in Elysium where we know it's safe."

Thunderwing made sure Windy had her immediate needs met, then said his good-byes.

She tried not to think about the creepy thing in the forest and focused on her new baby instead. Not sure how the child would take to the slices of meat, she grabbed a strip in her beak and placed it in her mouth as if it were a worm then let go. Mariah, hesitant at first, sucked it down only to have it get caught in her throat. Windy panicked. Instinctively, she reached into the baby's mouth with her beak and pulled out the sliver of meat. Mariah cried all the more and Windy drew a breath of relief.

"This is not going very well, little one, but it will work if we give it another go and I hold on to the other end. Let's try it again now, shall we?"

Windy dropped the end of a longer strip to the baby's mouth and held tightly to the opposite end. Mariah fumbled with the morsel in her hands and eventually got it to her mouth. Not having any teeth yet, she sucked on the meat.

It's working. Windy felt relieved. *The little dear is going to be just fine.*

Mariah gummed and sucked on the piece of meat until she absorbed most of its nutrients. When she started whining, Windy either turned the piece around or got a new strip.

Windy repeated this well into the night until her baby was satisfied and they both fell into a deep sleep.

Chapter 14

Much to Discover

"No, no, dear. It's peck one, feather two—peck one, feather two. The way you're going about it, it will all bunch up. That's good. Now you've got it."

Aunt Cloudcast showed Windy how to weave for her new baby. They used a pile of feathers to create Mariah's first clothes.

"Now, don't take any more feathers from yourself, dearie, you need to keep as many as you can grow. There are plenty of us donating, so no worries. Now, take another and let me watch you again."

As shown, Windy took a downy feather from the pile and, with her beak, punched a hole into the lower part of the quill.

"That's the way to do it, dear."

Windy took two other downy feathers, and slipped their quill ends through the small gap, thus hooking the three together.

"Let me see now. Ah yes, marvelous," Aunt Cloudcast said.

Windy bored a small hole in the quill ends of the two

she'd threaded through and slipped in two downy feathers, making seven feathers hooked together in a triangular shape.

"Marvelous, dear, just marvelous. Make sure they're even at the top. That's right. Now you'll want to 'peck one, feather one' for a while so it won't get too big too fast. Oh, and be sure to use the longer ones for the shoulder area. Marvelous."

Windy followed the pattern instructions, dictated by a watchful aunt, until a blanket of feathers fanned out in a long triangle.

"Aunty, do you think this will be long enough?" Windy was grateful for her aunt's help, even if she could be a bit overbearing at times. Windy never knew her mother, Windstar, the daughter of Screaming Eagle. She'd died in his wings shortly after laying the egg of her only child. Aunt Cloudcast missed her sister terribly and gladly checked in on Windy as often as possible.

"Only one way to find out, dearie. Let's take another peek at the child and see if she's awake. If she is, we can slip it around her. That will tell us for sure."

Windy lifted herself, exposing the delicate pink skin of her baby to the cold. A startling shiver shot through Mariah and caused her to suck in cold air. Her face scrunched up and she cried.

"Oh, dear. Well, she's awake now," Aunt Cloudcast said. "Here, try it on quickly before the darling gets too much of a chill and goes into a full-blown wail. The mountain knows we don't want another one of those now, do we, dear?"

"No, Aunty. I'm hurrying."

"Marvelous. Now start at the neck first, dearie, then wrap it under her arm and around her back and all the way to the front again."

"I know, Aunty."

"Here, let me hold the end while you work it."

Windy rolled Mariah to her stomach, wrapped the feathery shawl around, then rolled her to her back for the final fit in front. It came up short.

"I saw it right off, my dear," Aunt Cloudcast said, puffing her chest up with pride. "Just wanted you to see for yourself. And it would be best if you taper this end off for a better fit over the other shoulder so it can be fastened properly behind the neck."

Windy rolled her eyes and let out a breath. "Yes, Aunty."

"Marvelous, my dear, you do learn well. It's a good thing I know a thing or two about weaving. Don't know how you would have managed without me."

"I don't know either, Aunty."

Windy made all the proper adjustments and fastened the crude cloak behind Mariah's neck as her aunty suggested. It fitted. Mariah didn't shiver so much with the tightly woven feathers around her. Only her bare legs and arms poked through. Of course, Aunt Cloudcast knew that was coming too, but wanted Windy to figure it out on her own. Before the day was over, all arms and legs were covered in downy feathers.

"Oh my, that certainly improves the poor child's looks." Aunt Cloudcast said, happy with herself.

Windy checked her handiwork and decided that it would keep most of the cold air away from Mariah. By the end of the day she lay exhausted, not just from the weaving but also from dealing with her aunt for so long.

All in all, the day went well. Mariah had only one full-blown cry that made Aunt Cloudcast want to stuff the leftover feathers into the screaming mouth. Windy quickly found a strip of rabbit for Mariah to suck on, which appeased the child's hunger. For the most part, Windy found Mariah to be a good-natured baby who only cried when she had a reason.

Months passed and the eagles got used to the human child. Windy never lacked help and Mariah was well cared for. Often, the others would take turns sitting with her, watching and keeping her warm, while Windy took breaks to stretch her wings.

Spring came. Flowers bloomed in a full array of colors, and tall blades of grass waved in the breeze as if invisible hands brushed their tops. The aspen trees came to life with new buds sprouting into thousands of fluttering leaves, and songbirds sang in the branches. Even the bees woke from their sleep and filled the air with an excited 'first come, first served' battle with the hummingbirds for the new nectar.

As gently as a mother with lethal talons can, Windy took the feather-clad child in her grip. She felt the weight of the girl for balance and discovered the baby wasn't bothered being jostled around, so she took the chance.

For the first time since she'd rescued the child from the crows, Windy flew Mariah to the meadow by the lake's shore and let her explore so that she might feel the grass between her fingers. Mariah loved the water; she would slap her grass-stained hand into her reflection and squeal with delight.

The spring breeze soon turned to hot summer air. Often, the eagles congregated at the lake to watch Mariah, and they marveled at how easily she made friends with the squirrels and rabbits. It was especially fun to watch her play with the raccoons. Sometimes, they became a little rough with the baby and one of the eagles would have to fly in and peck the ruffians as a reminder. Her guardians always watched her closely, not just because of the raccoons, but also because of the rumors of some strange creature of music and smoke that lurked in the lower woods and mutilated animals then left them strewn about. So watchful eyes were more than casual.

The seasons continued to rotate, and Mariah grew stronger and more curious. By the second summer, she learned to walk by emulating the eagles—she stretched her arms out to her sides and waddled, making Windy very proud.

In her third summer, Mariah learned to run. She chased baby bunnies and scattered the birds that came to feast on grass seeds. A couple of years later, her animal friends included fawns and rabbits, and whenever possible, she'd cuddle up with the mountain lions.

She loved their looks, especially their soft coat of fur, in which she would bury her face. The cats, with their meticulous grooming, would rather not be bothered by anyone, let alone a fur lover like Mariah. It came to the point that they would perch themselves up on branches whenever they saw her coming.

Mariah spent most of her time with her best friend, Moonglider, a young eagle a year older than her. They grew up together on the cliffs, often visiting each other's nests. While Mariah learned to walk, Moonglider took her first rocky flight lessons. The beautiful eaglet had rich, dappled brown tones in her feathers, and golden eyes trimmed in yellow that were sharper than her mother's, Moonbeam. Moonglider stood five-feet tall and already surpassed the wingspan of a normal adult golden eagle by a good six feet, but she and the rest of the mountain eagles weren't normal.

The water was a natural draw for Mariah. Always warm, the lake became an irresistible invitation. The girl's zeal for the water many times caused Windy to pluck her out to safer ground. Mariah loved it, and Windy, other than some frazzled nerves, enjoyed it too.

More seasons passed, and Mariah grew gracefully into her twelfth summer.

One day, during the hot part of the day, she ventured to the western ridge that held Elysium valley in a bowl, like fresh salad ready to eat. At the top, she sat to rest on a moss-spotted rock next to a ponderosa pine. The cushioned forest floor of pine needles felt good to her bare feet, and pinecones, old fallen trees, and aspen added to the mystic atmosphere of the forest.

Mariah pulled in her feet and laced her fingers around her knees. She sat, silent, with her back to the tree and closed her eyes, listening to the sounds around her. She first became aware of her heart pounding in her ears, but the pounding of the waterfall below drowned out most of that. The warm breeze brushed the trees, making a mournful sigh. Squirrels chattered, woodpeckers pecked, and bees in search of wildflowers buzzed. The grating sound of crows cawing deep in the woods made her cringe. She didn't know why, but she had a distinct dislike for crows.

Suddenly, something swooped in from nowhere and stopped right in front of her face with a thundering *'brrrrr.'* If it wasn't for the tree she leaned against, Mariah would have flinched right off the rock, but instead she hit her head on its trunk.

A clipped cry of surprise escaped her. Mariah held her head and, through a squinted eye, peeked up at the threatening sound. In spite of her pain, her eyes lit up and she leaned forward. "I don't believe it," she whispered with crossed eyes as wide as her opened mouth.

In midair, inches from her face, fluttered the smallest hummingbird she'd ever seen. About the size of the end of her thumb, its wings moved so fast that they seemed almost invisible. The bright red throat told her it was male, and he was so young he didn't even have a whistle yet. Mariah giggled through the subsiding pain and watched the little hummer hover before her. With a few flicks of his tongue, the hummer turned his pebble-sized head from side to side, studying what the squirrels were complaining about.

Mariah rubbed her head and spoke in the only language she knew—the eagle's. "Hey, little feller, where'd you come from?"

She plucked a wildflower from beside the rock and held it out to him. "Here you go, you cute little feller. Take a load off your wings and have a sip."

The baby hummingbird swooped in on the flower. Its tiny head moved back and forth, eyeing the token, then bent forward for a taste. "Cheep—cheep." The hummer flicked his gray tongue in and out through the point of his black beak.

Mariah instantly fell in love. "Oh, you darling little feller," she squeaked. "You can eat from my hand any time you want. Yes, you can."

The hummer touched its miniature toes to Mariah's hand and brought its rapid wings to a stop, tucking them neatly to his sides.

"Ahh," she sighed. "You precious little feller. What a cute little, little … that's it! I'll call you Feller. How cute. You don't mind if I call you that, do you, Feller?"

The baby hummingbird paid no attention and continued jabbing its toothpick-sharp beak in and out of the flower.

"How do you do, Feller, my name is Mariah." She reached out with her finger, which loomed bigger than the bird itself, and stroked his soft green feathers.

Feller raised his head, licked his beak, and stared into the face of the smiling, freckled girl.

Mariah slipped her finger underneath Feller's golden belly and lifted him up for a better look, but he flew back to the flower. She slid her finger back under him and pulled him away. Again, he flew back to the flower. Always one to tease, she pulled the flower away right before he reached it.

Feller followed, neck stretched forward.

Mariah stepped down from the rock and continued her backwards retreat.

He advanced on the flower.

She turned her body in a circle and giggled.

He chased the flower and chirped.

She kept spinning and laughed harder.

He chirped and sped faster.

She got dizzy.

He got thirsty.

She got weak from laughing so hard.

He finally caught the flower and, in flight, dipped his beak.

She crumbled to the ground, squealing, as the wobbly world spun through her head.

Feller, the clear winner of the game, took his place on Mariah's hand, taking in the last bit of nectar.

"Oh Feller, you're too much for me. You're hurting my sides." She laughed.

An eagle swooped in casually and landed on the rock where Mariah first sat. The girl was rolling on the ground, pine needles stuck everywhere in her hair and feathered garment, and a baby hummingbird licking at her ears.

"Ah, what seems to be the problem this time, Mariah? Gone and picked on someone bigger than yourself one *toooo* many times, didn't you?"

Mariah looked up at Moonglider and tried to talk through the giggles. "Help, Moon! I'm being licked to death by a hummer."

Moon couldn't help but laugh with her.

As quickly as the hummingbird had appeared, he vanished. Mariah sat up, brushed strands of hair from her face, and looked around, perplexed. Moon searched as well, until Mariah pointed at her and laughed even harder.

"What?" Moon demanded. "What is it? Stop laughing at me like that. What?"

Mariah couldn't stop long enough to tell her, but it wasn't necessary. Moon looked up, and locked eyes with the hummer. Feller was so light and small that Moon hadn't felt the little bird perched between her eyes.

Mariah and Moon made a new friend and the valley would never again be the same.

Only one thing did Mariah love more than baby hummingbirds, riding on an eagle's back—the thrill, the rush, the invigorating ups and downs—simply an adventure not to be missed.

"Come on, Moon. Come on, Feller." Mariah gasped through her giggles. She picked herself up from the soft floor of pine needles and jumped onto Moon's back. Feller perched on Mariah's head.

Moon had grown used to Mariah climbing on for rides. She liked taking the girl airborne, if only to hear her squeal through daring acrobatics. During flight, Moon often tried to do something unexpected, but this time Mariah had an unexpected turn for Moon.

When Moon swooped up the waterfall, Mariah sprang from her back with a wild scream. *"Wahooo!"* She sailed headlong into the crashing falls and disappeared into the churning foam below.

Moon couldn't believe Mariah would do such a crazy thing. She circled a few times nearer the water, as did Feller, but Mariah never came up.

"Do you see her?" Moonglider shouted to Feller.

"Chirp–squeak–squeak–chirp!" Feller twitched his head back and forth.

Moonglider's heart beat wildly with fear as she circled again. "Help! Someone—help! She's drowning!"

One more fruitless pass and Moon panicked, banking hard up the towering cliffs; she'd never beat her wings more feverishly. "Help! Anyone, please help!"

Like hornets dispatching from their hives, the eagles spewed into the air. Moonglider pushed hard with her wings and met the first eagles with the frightening news. As the news spread, the eagles tucked wings and one by one rifled to the lake. The air filled with the screams of diving eagles.

When Windy heard the news, her heart nearly faltered. Memories of crows picking at her daughter stirred her to action. Her baby was in trouble again and this time she feared it might be fatal.

Windy didn't remember descending to the lake; the panic blurred the flight. Eagles make wild attempts at diving under the water to search for the girl. Windy never liked the idea of immersing herself in the water but showed no hesitation now—none of the eagles did.

She lowered herself onto the lake with her wings spread and floated on its rippled surface. She thrust her head through the churning foam, desperately searching past the bubbles, lifting her head just long enough to take breaths. Eagles stormed everywhere, searching for Mariah. Feller darted about as well, but all he found were downy feathers littering the water.

"Do you see her anywhere?" Windy's composure began to unravel.

"Why'd she go and do a thing like that?" Aunt Cloudcast scolded.

"No one could have survived that." Thunderwing said.

"I told you years ago, Windy," Windstorm shouted tactlessly to her sister, "take the girl to the man-village and leave her."

"What hope is there?" Trekker's wings felt as heavy as his heart.

"There is no hope, none at all." In all his years, Screaming Eagle never gave up this easily—the world without Hope affected even the eagles.

"I knew something like this might happen." Moonbeam reprimanded her daughter, Moonglider.

"I'm sorry." Moonglider sat on the beach shivering as her tears fell. "I didn't know she would do something like that. I should have never gone near the waterfall."

"She's gone …" Windy, crushed, accepted the awful fact.

The birds flew aimlessly or gathered by the shores of the lake—not knowing what to do or where to go—their minds numb and their heads hung in cooing sobs.

Mariah was dead.

Mariah made a smooth entry into the base of the waterfall. Bubbles tickled her bare arms and legs and a trail of thousands more squiggled behind her. She screamed into the water, fascinated with the liquid sound of her voice. A powerful undertow jerked her back into the turbulence just as she started to swim toward the surface. The current dragged her down—down beneath the pounding waterfall. She flailed out of control and the weight of the water slammed her to the rocky bottom.

The violent turmoil knocked out what little air she had in her lungs and water rushed in, choking her. She panicked and struggled, fighting to break free, but the falling water kept her pinned. Hope leaked from Mariah in the same way that it leaked from the world. Why fight any longer when it was easier to give up?

Just when she gave herself over to the power of the water, the undertow spewed her out of the confusion. She floated limp in the current. About to pass out, her vision faded, then out from nowhere, thousands of silvery objects circled around her, tickling at her arms and legs, and lifted her lifeless body up to the surface until her head pushed above the lake.

Water spewed from her, and through coughing fits, she gasped in spiced air. She had neither strength nor desire to tread water, yet she floated and breathed life until her lungs cleared.

It took some time in the enriched atmosphere for her to gain her composure and realize that thousands of fish hatchlings were keeping her afloat. Curious, she scooped a hand through the water, lifted out a cluster of little squiggling babies, and watched them flip back into the water. She smiled and scooped another handful of fish— the tragedy just moments before forgotten in her curiosity.

She found herself in a choppy pool with thundering sheets of water tumbling behind her and a ragged stone wall with deep ledges towering before. Evidently, the dive had propelled her behind the waterfall into a secluded grotto. The waterfall splintered sunlight like a prism into hundreds of dancing lights that flickered against the amphitheater-like walls.

"What is this place?" Mariah swiped strands of hair from her face, swam to the nearest ledge, and lifted herself out onto warm rocks. She sat breathing deep of the spiced air. It brought to mind wildflowers mixed with aspen and something else she couldn't pick out. The more she breathed, the less her lungs ached, and the clearer her mind became.

Colored lights danced all around her. Impulsively, she slapped at a bouncing light on the stone slab next to her. Like the bubbles rising in the water, a giggle bubbled up from her. She slapped at a light again, rocked herself to her knees, and reached for one in midair. They seemed so real that she believed if she caught one she could eat it. With the smell of spice making her hungry, the game was on.

She bounced to her feet and grabbed at the reflections—all eluded her grasp. She tried again to trap the gaily-colored crystals of light against the back wall, to no avail. Through all the jumping, squatting, twisting, and turning, Mariah created a dance of her own. She climbed her way up the ledges, leaping at the gems until she found herself far above the surface of the pool.

Under the top of the falls, she stood and felt the power of the water as it poured over the cliff above. Behind the sheet of falling water, shadowed images flew about. A mischievous look crossed her face. She pressed herself back against the water-streaked cliff. All her muscles flexed—ready and poised.

The eagles' search party caught the attention of the animals that lived in the valley and they gathered at the lake. Even Puma, the large mountain lion, woke from his slumber. He needed a drink anyway, so he slipped on down to the lake to see what all the fuss was about. "What's going on?" he growled.

Trekker flew by in a panic. "Mariah! She's—"

"Wahooo!" A long, wild cry rang from the top of the waterfall. Mariah sailed headlong through the rushing waters, shot into the midst of the circling eagles, made a half roll and grabbed her knees for a cannonball splash.

The animals were amused, thinking the eagles and Mariah were putting on some kind of special show. The eagles, however, couldn't believe it was Mariah until she bobbed halfway out of the water, flipping her wet hair behind.

"Yes!" she shouted and waved to the eagles and animals on the shore. "Here I am!" She giggled and splashed about.

Screaming Eagle plucked her up by her shoulders and flew her to the safety of dry ground.

"What'd you do that for?" Mariah asked.

"Young girl," he said, "you're in a lot of trouble."

Everyone gathered around the girl who stood dripping in her matted feathers. Windy threw both wings around her, sobbing with relief.

"It's all right, Momma." Mariah wasn't sure what all the fuss was about. Feller hovered in front of her, chirping frantically.

Once Windy knew Mariah was okay, her fear turned to ire and she paced back and forth. "What in the name of Misty do you think you were doing, little girl? Look at you. Your clothes are ruined, and I'll be up all night with Aunt Cloudcast repairing what you've damaged." She leaned in, gave a wide-eyed look of dread, and whispered harshly, *"Aunt Cloudcast."*

"I was just having some fun," Mariah tried to explain, pointing to the waterfall. "There's this cave on the other—"

"Child," Windy scolded, "I don't care anything about a cave. I only care that you made us think you had drowned and were forever lost to us."

"But Momma ..." Mariah pulled a few strands of wet hair from her mouth and hooked them behind her ear.

"No 'buts,' child! You must never go where we are not able to help. Do you understand?"

Mariah searched her family and saw faces of anger, concern, and relief. She wondered if human parents from the tribe were just as protective.

Screaming Eagle's imposing reptile stare cut deeper than usual. "Whippoorwill snapper," he muttered to himself.

Windy's angry demeanor broke and she sighed, changing her tone. "Are you okay?"

Mariah lowered her head, embarrassed with all the animals listening in. "Yes, Momma," she spoke softly. "I was just having fun."

"I know, darling. I guess we all didn't know how much we could have lost until we thought you were gone." Windy looked around. Everyone stared at them. "Come, dear," she whispered, "what do you say we go home? We can get a bite to eat, dry off, and settle our nerves a bit. It's still a beautiful day, and you can tell me all about this cave while I repair your clothes. I really would love to hear."

Mariah threw her arms around Windy's neck and rubbed her nose back and forth on her beak—the kiss of eagles. At that moment, she knew there wasn't anything

Windy wouldn't have done for her. The honesty in her affections, the way she snuggled unabashedly, always drove Windy crazy with motherly love.

"Is that all there's going to be?" said Puma, lying in the sun, eyes half closed. "Was hardly worth the drink of water." He licked his paws.

Mariah climbed onto her mother's back and waved to the animals. Windy took a few hops, flapped her wings, and made off to the opal skies. The others followed suit, relieved that it had been a false alarm.

The other animals wandered off, still musing over the dance of the eagles and Mariah's surprise dive. They would remember it for a long time to come.

Windy flew Mariah back to their nest, and Mariah had to bite her lip to keep from laughing after overhearing her mother whisper:

"This is going to be a long summer."

Chapter 15
Creature Encounter

"Careful, you're going to wake him." Moon whispered, trying not to laugh.

"Almost there. Stop pushing." Mariah snapped back.

"I'm telling you, if you wake him, I'm leaving you behind."

"No you don't. We're in this together. Now hold me, so I don't fall."

"*Shhh*—quiet ..." the young eagle said. "He just moved ..."

They made more of a racket trying not to laugh than just laughing aloud.

With two feathers pinched between thumb and finger, Mariah stretched her arm over a rocky ledge where an old eagle lay comfortably napping in his nest, twitching his wings to the dreams dancing before his eyelids.

Slowly, carefully, the two ends of the feathers reached Mariah's grandfather, who snored peacefully in his nest of well-worn sticks. A master nest builder, his nest was tightly woven and hard, just the way he liked it. Every day he took a snooze in the middle of the afternoon. Never before had he any cause to be concerned.

Still trying to hold in a laugh, Mariah synchronized herself with his breathing, waiting for the right moment. He took long breaths and snored loudly with powerful exhalations and deep inhalations. It was her move—now or never.

Quickly, when the inhale reached its pinnacle, she wedged the ends of the feathers straight into his two snort-holes. There was a short struggle of breath and the sound of air leaking, then ...

Pop–pop!

The feathers shot straight up into the air then floated down in lazy circles.

Mariah clapped a hand over her mouth to hold back the laughter and held Moon's beak closed with the other. Her eyebrows arched while muffled snickers escaped.

Screaming Eagle only blew a few shots of air, muttered something about quieting the squirrels, and then adjusted his wings before continuing his noisy nap.

The two troublemakers watched the twirling feathers flutter their way down the cliffs in perfect circles. While Moon watched the feathers' looping flight, Mariah yanked two fresh ones from her backside. She gave a muted shriek then slugged Mariah with her wing.

Mariah paid no attention. "Hold me tight, Moon," she whispered. "I'm going back in."

The vibration of the old bird's snoring rattled two sticks from his nest together, making it sound like a katydid in song. Mariah gave Moon a sidelong glance, with her bottled laughter on the verge of rupture.

Through stinging tears of restrained giddiness, Moon took hold of the back of Mariah's feathered clothes while she leaned again over to the unsuspecting sleeper.

Screaming Eagle's breathing rattled deep and steady.

Subdued chuckles clipped Moonglider's breathing.

Mariah held her breath and gritted her teeth.

The sticks chirped.

Moon chuckled and heaved.

Mariah snickered.

At the peak of Screaming Eagle's inhale, Mariah fitfully inserted the feathers, almost missing the mark.

Moon chuckled too hard, lost her grip and sent Mariah slamming head first, full weight, into her grandfather.

Screaming Eagle woke abruptly, but not before he executed a perfect two-feather launch. "Dang nab-it!" the old bird barked, his sleepy, crossed eyes focused on feathers twirling past his vision.

Moon panicked. "Now you've done it."

Mariah's grin changed to fright. No one laughed now.

"Jump, Mariah." Moonglider leaped off the cliff in front of Screaming Eagle's nest. "Jump, now!"

Mariah, heart beating fast, flew off the ledge and caught Moon as she sped by. The momentum of Mariah's leap propelled them swiftly away, and their unbridled laughter trailed in the air. They couldn't believe the look on Screaming Eagle's face or the fact that they'd escaped by the skin of their feathers.

"Dang whippoorwill snappers!" Screaming Eagle shouted after them, trying to act madder than he was. "See if I disturb your rest sometime!"

They knew Screaming Eagle to be a gruff old bird who had an air of no foolishness about him. What they didn't know was that he really didn't mind them singling him out like that. In a certain way he liked the attention—even if it did end up making him look a bit undignified. The two youths made him feel younger than he had in a long time. He may never have admitted it, but to him it was worth the shenanigans.

"Wished I'd of thought of that one when I was young." The old bird chuckled to himself as he watched the two soar away in a crooked line. For a moment, he was back in his mother's nest, remembering his carefree youth and thinking of the rotten things he used to do.

A spring breeze blew upon him, and a chill penetrated his old bones. He snuggled his wings tight and tucked his head inside one of them, his mind wandering in happier times. Before long, his whole bed was once again a singing nest of katydids.

Four more years passed, and Mariah outgrew or wore-out her suit of feathers a couple of dozen times. It became such a routine to fashion new clothes that Windy showed Mariah how to weave her own. With the dexterity of the teenager's fingers, she had the ability to make short work of what took Windy a long and agonizing time to accomplish. But Mariah always turned her nose up at chores, acting as if they were some kind of punishment. She submitted half-heartedly, but would rather have been chasing blackbirds or playing in the water. Windy eventually decided it was easier to do things herself, though she wondered more than once: *who's training whom?*

For the most part Mariah, Moon, and Feller became inseparable. Between pranks, they flew below the protective banks of Elysium Valley and visited the village by the Misty River. Fly-bys only, for Mariah felt too shy to meet the villagers face to face.

Except for the color of her skin and hair, Mariah looked like them and was naturally curious. She'd ask her mother about how she came to be with the eagles, but Windy would only tease: "I saw something glittering on the water one day, and I thought it was a beautiful fish, so I plucked it out, but instead of the fish, there you were. Ever since, I've been wanting to just eat you up!" And she would nuzzle Mariah's belly with her beak until the little girl would forget about her question and giggle.

As the girl got older, Windy revealed bits and pieces of Mariah's puzzled life, but never anything satisfying. The most she got out of her mother was that she was rescued from the cold of winter.

The human tribe at the foot of Elysium fascinated her, especially their complicated language. Their words sounded richer than the squeaks and squawks of her eagle language, and she wanted to know more—but not today.

Right now her fascination lay with the waterfall and the hidden cave beyond its veil. Nearly four years had passed since she'd visited the secret grotto of lights and spice. It drew her, and captivated her every waking moment. Her mom had forbidden her to go near the falls again, so she'd put it out of her mind, but now that she had grown older and felt more certain of herself, she turned her attention once again to the falls.

"Hey, Moon." Mariah sat down in the long grass by the crashing waterfall and stared into its hypnotic flow.

Feller flew to a patch of flowers while Moonglider strolled in the grass, watching bugs—a new interest of hers.

"Yeah?"

"Been thinkin'."

"Oh no."

"Yep, I have."

"What this time?"

"Oh, you know, stuff."

"That's the stuff stuff's made of—like what?"

"Oooh … how to get back behind the waterfall again."

"Like I said, 'Oh no.'"

"Gotta do it."

"Sure, go right ahead. Feller and I will watch."

"Nope, you're gonna help."

"I'm gonna do nothing of the sort."

"Oh yes, you are."

Moon poked her head up over the grass. "No way, not this bird. Last time, you had all of Elysium in a panic. Your Ma will kill you and then she'll come lookin' for me. Uh-uh." She shook her head. "Better think of something else, and fast." She went back to observing her bugs.

"Yeah, but things are different now."

"Different? Nothing's different except you're sixteen and a little crazy. But we'll wait. In a few more years you'll be as good as new. Besides, Thunder and Trekker are on to you about something, not to mention your grandpa keeping a tighter eye our way too—doesn't seem to trust us for some reason."

"I know, that's why I've been thinkin'."

"Thinkin'. There goes that 'we're headed for trouble' word again. Okay, Mariah, whatcha been thinkin'?"

"First, I'm thinkin' we'll send the two watch-birds on a little investigating trip right about when Grandpa takes his nap. Ma and the others are usually looking for dinner at that time, so that leaves me free to take a long-overdue visit back to the water cave."

"Investigating trip? What's interesting enough for those two to wanna go investigate?"

"Haven't you heard?"

"Guess not."

"There's some kind of creature in the woods."

Moonglider stopped again and poked her head up from the grass in curiosity. "Creature?"

"*Creeatuure*," Mariah whispered hauntingly, eyes wide.

Feller overheard the conversation and flew to Mariah's shoulder, and gave her his complete attention—sipping nectar would have to wait.

Moon's left eye closed halfway in suspicious thought. "What sort of creature? There're lots of odd creatures in the woods, you know."

"Yeah, like Feller!" Mariah gave a tickle to the hummingbird's green belly right below his bright red throat.

"Yeah, I'd watch out for that dangerous 'creature' if I were you," Moon added, making her way to Mariah. "He can be scary."

"You know, he did come dangerously close to poking my eye once."

"That's nothing, he whistled in my ear and it rang most of the day—couldn't hear Ma calling me home for dinner. Got me in trouble, *you little crow.*"

Feller was usually amused with the teasing but something had struck him deeply when Mariah mentioned the creature. "Squeak, squawk—chirp, squeak!"

Mariah stopped joking. "You heard about it too, Feller?"

"Chirp, chirp—squeak squawk."

"I heard more than that from Puma," Mariah said

matter-of-factly. "Saw him a few weeks ago racing over the ridge as if he was chasing something, or something bigger was chasing him. A bear, I thought. Ran right up that ponderosa over there by the aspens. Didn't even stop to rest on the first branch like he usually does—went straight to the top. I knew something had to be wrong, so I ran to see if he was okay."

"Did you find out anything?" Moon asked. "He's always been a hard one to get a straight answer from. At least for me, anyway."

"Yeah, me too. At first, he didn't say anything, but he sure smelled bad. It was like fire without the smoke. It made me want to hold my nose to keep from sneezing."

"Wow, it isn't like Puma to smell or look anything less than perfect."

"Yeah, and he wasn't looking so good either—like he'd been swatted a few times by a bear. Thought he got too close again to Kodiak and her cub. You just don't do that, and Puma knows better. She can be a mean bear when it comes to her babies. So best to leave her alone until they're grown, then she'll even share her berries with you if you want."

"Berries? No way, she's never done that with me."

"Ya gotta ask nice, Moon. If you do it right, she can make you feel like you're one of her cubs—she'll stuff ya good."

"Chirp–chirp–chirp!"

"I'm getting back to it, Feller. You be careful around her too, ya hear?"

"So what did you do to get Puma to talk?"

"It took some time for him to calm down. All he did was growl, *'Liar—Liar—Liar.'* He was quite upset and his ears were flat back like he really meant it."

"No kiddin'? What did you do?"

"I climbed up to the bottom branch—you know, where he usually rests. I was going up to see him, but he snarled something horrible and I stopped right there. Figured I would wait for him to calm down a bit. He eventually did, but he was still plenty mad. Took me a while to get anything out of him. But with cats, ya gotta be patient; there's just no hurrying them."

"Well, maybe if you would hurry?" Moon said. "Come on, what'd he say about the creature?"

"I'm getting to that. I told him if he'd come down out of the tree—'cause the branch was biting into me something horrible—I would scratch behind his ears, and he could tell me all about it. He likes it when I scratch behind his ears—can hardly resist it unless, of course, it's under his chin. It calms—"

"Mariah!"

"All right, already! Anyway, he never would come down, so I climbed up a few more branches, and then I saw it."

"Saw what?"

"He had blood on his shoulder, all matted up, and the fur around his eyes was soaking wet. I asked him if he was hurt. He said yes, but I knew the wounds weren't the reason for his tears—he can be a tough cat."

Mariah pulled a grass shoot from the ground and nibbled its end before continuing. "You know what he told me?"

"What?"

"'I'm afraid.' That's what he said. Can you imagine Puma being afraid of anything?"

"I didn't know Puma was a fraidy-cat."

"Puma wasn't afraid like that, Moon. He wasn't even hiding, like I first thought. He was on the lookout. I tried to get him to relax, but he kept looking around as if he expected something to come up into Elysium Valley. Believe me, if anything did he would have done something about it right then and there.

"'Stay there and don't move,' he whispered down to me. 'Something evil has come to the mountain.'

"Evil? I thought some foreign men were prowling about, like they did years ago, before Misty took care of them. But he wasn't kidding, you guys, there was something awful wandering around out there. He said something I'll never forget: 'A man walks on two legs and animals walk on four, but this *Thing*,' and he emphasized *Thing* with a snarl, 'is made of gems and walks on three.'"

"Three?" Moon moved in front of Mariah and settled herself down in the grass. "Three legs? What in the name of Misty walks on three legs and is made of colored stones?"

"Beats me, Moon. But it gets weirder. When Puma snarled, I noticed one of his fangs missing—broken off. He shook all over when I asked him about the fang and the blood on his shoulder. 'I attacked the Liar!' he growled."

"Liar—there's that word again. What lies was he talking about?"

"That's the scary part for me. Puma didn't go into a lot of detail. All he said was that a creature like a man, but not a man, stalked the mountain with a voice beautiful to listen to. Beautiful enough that it made Puma want to believe its lies."

"Lies, lies, lies! Mariah, what lies?"

"Lies about Misty." she shot back. "This thing told Puma that Misty was greedy and was holding him captive. It promised Puma a mountain of his own if he wanted, to rule other mountain cats and animals too, and that it would show him how. It promised him that it would make him happy and that there was more than one mountain around that could satisfy. It said that it would help him escape from this murderous Misty, the taker of innocent lives, but he'd have to be a follower of the creature."

Moon seemed shocked. "Puma may be lazy, but he's no fool. I mean, no one's happier anywhere else than here with Misty?"

"Yeah, thank the Mountain for that. The creature sure made those promises sound possible to him. After it called Misty a killer, Puma recognized the deceiver it was and demanded that it leave, but Puma said it felt like trying to demand the river to stop flowing. So he attacked it. That's all I know."

"Good for Puma. Where is he now? I haven't seen him for awhile. Is he all right?"

"Other than feeling a bit ashamed that he considered those lies as truth, I don't think his wounds were that bad. I last saw Puma that same day when he finally came down from the tree … said he was going to patrol the woods. I haven't seen him since.

"I told Momma about it right away. She got upset when I told her and said it wasn't good to spread rumors, especially lies about Misty. Told me to keep it to myself and let the rumor die, so I did—'til now.

"I'm a little worried about Puma, you guys, that's why I think it would be great for Thunder and Trekker to go looking for him. They're good at things like that. Besides, I really do want to know if Puma's all right and if he's found out anything more. Or maybe they'll come across the creature themselves?

"And while they're doing that, guess what we're going to do?" Mariah's eyes got big.

"Don't tell me—go to the cave?"

"Yes! It's perfect, don't you think? Come on, Moon, you're the only one who can help."

"Oh Mariah, what kind of trouble will you think of next?" Moon sighed. "Fine, to the cave."

The next day, about the time Screaming Eagle took his afternoon naps, Moonglider carried Mariah to see Thunderwing and Trekker. The two cousins, in the prime of their young adult lives, prided themselves on looking out for the inhabitants of Elysium. Misty didn't need the help but appreciated the gesture greatly, taking it as a sign that the eagles believed in the mountain and wanted to preserve the good there.

The news of Puma's encounter with the creature concerned the eagle cousins. They told Mariah they'd known for a number of years about some strange thing prowling the forest but they'd never found it, only the creepy evidence of the animals it'd killed, strewn about the hills.

Mariah felt that a battle of fear shadowed the two brave eagles when they raced off to investigate the borders of Elysium.

Feller, known to be a bold bird, especially for his size, buzzed brazenly after Thunderwing and Trekker.

Mariah rode Moon who flew aimlessly while they waited for her mother to go hunting with the rest. When the skies were finally clear of eagles, they broke into a tucked dive.

"Go, Moon, go!"

Moonglider loved to dive. The wind fluttering her feathers against her skin and gravity pulling at her gave her a rush. She found it liberating to be in complete control as the ground reached to claim her life. She longed for excuses like this to stretch her limits.

"Faster, Moon. It's got to be faster!"

She pulled out her wings, gave a few hard flaps, then tucked them in tight. They dropped fast, faster than she'd ever gone before.

Their hearts beat wildly. Tears—from the air rushing against their eyes—gathered at the corners, blurring their vision. Lake Elysium came up quicker than Moon expected. Just as she started to think of the consequences of their speed, Mariah squealed.

"Faasterr!"

Mariah held on so tight that the front of Moon's wings went numb. Mariah had every bit of confidence in her, but Moon's confidence took a dive right along with her fall. She'd gone past the point where she could have comfortably leveled out.

She expanded her wings and struggled for lift. Her neck stretched forward and wings flexed vertically, but it wasn't enough. She couldn't feel her limbs, and her control failed. For a moment, she seriously thought of giving up and letting herself hit the water with full force. *The impact will make a great ending*, she thought—a fitting way to go out with a splash. Then her hopelessness passed.

"Pull!" she screamed over Mariah's squeals. The water was coming up fast. "Mariah—pull. Pull my wings up—*NOW!*"

Mariah pulled back on Moon's wings, still squealing.

"Harder, Mariah. We're going to crash—pull harder!"

Mariah dug deep into Moon's wings and yanked them to vertical. Air pounded hard against the wings and Moonglider's belly feathers skipped across the lake's surface, spraying water behind. Slowly, they arced parallel with the lake and sped straight for the waterfall.

Moon felt Mariah's knees tight against her, saw her hands lift into the rushing air, and heard her giggle. Barely back in control, Moon's heart hammered at the close call. The pounding of the waterfall flooded her ears with thunder. It was coming up quick!

"Now!" screamed Mariah.

Moon banked hard to the left, directly in front of the falls. Mariah released her knees and threw herself straight into the avalanche.

"Wahooo!" And she was gone.

Chapter 16
If Walls Could Talk

Clouded eyes stared blankly up the steep embankment of rocks and trees that led to Elysium Valley. Flies buzzed a thick tangle of excitement in the stench-filled air. An object shot through the middle of the mass of flies; a few fell from the air. Again, the object—a giant by any fly's standard—zipped through. A few more flies fell to the ground, but the hummingbird's charge left the swarm unaffected, and it continued its feast.

Feller found himself between panic and steaming fury. He couldn't believe what he saw past the thicket of raging insects: It was beyond barbaric—a vision of diabolical insanity.

The flies yielded in a wide orb around his rushing wings while he hovered before the face whose eyes would see no more. In a fit of helplessness, Feller spun in oblong circles, chirping his frustration. But he could do nothing; he was simply too small.

A few spins more and he sped off into the sun-streaked air. He didn't care about the beauty of the forest or the flowers sprouting in the shade of branches, nor did he care about the abundance of sweet nectar gathered there. He had no appetite; the bees could have it all to themselves. He had to get Trekker and Thunderwing, and quick.

Mariah shot through the waterfall like an arrow, and dove straight into the pool beyond. She breached the surface with thousands of fish hatchlings boiling at her sides. With a flick of her head, her wet hair whipped neatly out of her face. The air smelled rich in spice just the way she remembered, and the afternoon sun shone through the water in dancing colored lights.

She took a deep breath of the rich air. "I'm back." Her voice echoed in the grotto.

With a few kicks, Mariah reached the ledge and pulled herself from the water, her heart still pounding from the rush of adrenalin.

She looked around, and felt as if she'd never left. Everything seemed exactly as she remembered. It would be difficult to leave this place, but she'd promised Moonglider she would be out before her mother came back from her hunt.

She stood and looked around the natural auditorium, observing for the first time what lay beyond the dancing lights. Crystals spotted the grotto walls, sparkling when the dotted lights floated across their surfaces. They glowed with a warm, delicate radiance as if they were inhaling with each touch of a light. She went to the back of the cave and placed each hand on a crystal. They felt warm to the touch. Then she noticed something else: mushrooms grew in the cracks of the walls.

Mariah loved mushrooms and ate them whenever she

found them in the woods. She picked one the size of her hand with its umbrella opened wide and nibbled its edge. A satisfied grin spread across her face. Somehow, she knew it would have the flavor of the spiced air. She walked slowly along the wall, following the scent of spice while she nibbled her mushroom and traced the glowing crystals with her hand. Soon, she found a glowing hole the size of her fist about shoulder height in the wall.

Wind hissed deep within the gap. She peered in. The same crystals that studded the walls of the grotto lined the hole, but they shone even brighter. A warm breeze hit her face, and her nostrils ached to take another breath of the balmy air.

She turned, put her back against the warm wall and melted to the floor, basking in the dancing colored lights and enjoying all that her nose inhaled. She closed her eyes and finished her mushroom, savoring each bite. The day felt perfect.

In the relaxed atmosphere, she let her imagination drift to other places. She dreamed of flowers, sunshine, and moonlight shimmering off the lake on a warm summer evening. The rushing of the waterfall reminded her of gentle breezes through the trees, and the sound she heard while riding the wind with Moon. Then she envisioned herself with wings of her own.

Why is it that I'm so different from the rest? Why must I be human? I want to fly and have beautiful feathers too.

She stood up and spoke aloud. "I want to dance on the wind!" She sang the words with her arms spread like wings.

Her imagination lifted her to the sky above the mountains where she pretended the rushing of the falls to be the wind against her face. She glided by Misty's forest, smelling the richest pine in the world, and pretended the droplets from the waterfall were actually mouthfuls of clouds.

"*Wheee!*" she squealed in her daydream. She envisioned the clouds clinging to her golden-brown feathers, leaving her washed coat a radiant white. "Look! I'm queen of the eagles," she shouted, and turned in lazy circles.

A gurgling voice called her name …

"*Ma—ri—ah …*"

"Here I am," Mariah said. "I'm your queen and this cave my throne."

"*Ma—ri—ah …*" it called again.

"Speak, my love, and I will fly with you forever!" she replied with glee.

Again, the earthy voice called her name. Mariah stopped abruptly mid-twirl, and her eyes shoot open. The voice sounded too real for play. Afraid to move, she turned her eyes from side to side, looking for something, but not finding.

"*Ma—ri—ah …*"

There it was again. The hair on the back of her neck stood on end. She couldn't doubt it this time—the voice was real, and it came from—she turned with a startled cry, but found no one there. She scanned the walls. But wait … there! A stream of mist flowed from the lighted crystal hole. Her eyes fixed on the spot. She dared not blink. Then she heard her name again as the vapor accentuated each syllable.

"*Ma—ri—ah …*"

She didn't know what to do, or what to say. Her skin felt like gooseflesh all over. "Wh—what? Who's there?" she barely squeaked it out.

"*Ma—ri—ah …*" The voice called again from the

crack. *"I have waited a long time for you to be queen, too. Time is not ready for you yet—but soon."*

"Who are you?" Her voice held a slight note of demand. Slowly, the vapor puffed out a riddle:

"I am ancient by your standards, an infant by Time's
My side's too steep, no one can climb.
A master of destruction, a servant of peace,
My tears are like fire, my mouth like a breeze.
My skin is of stone, my heart is of gold;
My eyes see everything, a door's threshold.
I shake like a leaf, my roots deeper than a tree;
Tell me now, Mariah, do you know who I might be?"

Everything seemed so strange, so frightening and alluring all at the same time. She stood straight, gathered her composure, and pondered the riddle.

"Misty?" she whispered. "Misty, is that you?"

"It is as you say," the mist puffed out.

She took a step back, her mind grasping the reality. "It is you. And you're talking to me?" She reflected a moment. "Momma says you don't talk very often."

"Yes, it has been a long time."

"But you talked to her once, didn't you?"

From within the hole, a long stream of vapor poured.

"Yes. She was about your age, curious and special, and I showed her many things that would come. I don't always reveal what is going on around me, and what I show, I'm selective of. One vision was of you; the other, too mean and cruel to share.

"The world has become increasingly evil, Mariah. Even as we speak, wickedness has reached its long arm to the skirts of my domain. There is great trouble brewing."

"Have foreigners come to the mountain like Momma told me they did once?"

"There is an intruder, yes, but more dangerous. Something worse—there is disruptive talk, mistrust, and lies. By the spread of untruths, their faith in me is shaken. There is trouble, Mariah. Will you speak on my behalf?"

"Speak to whom about what? I don't know what to do or say."

"Go to both beast and man. Simply tell them about me. Tell them that I am alive, that I care, and that I am watching over them. Tell them I do not lie or deceive but that I am truth. Tell them ... Mariah, please, tell them I love them and that I haven't forgotten."

The sincerity of Misty's words crushed her heart. She drew herself closer to the wall. She placed her hands on either side of the hole and leaned her face into it. "I have always loved you, Misty," she whispered sincerely. "You are the Mountain of my mother and the creator of my home. I have always known you. I wouldn't ever want to be far from you. I would say what's already in my heart and no less. What lies could ever be told of you, I cannot imagine."

"Mariah, there has been a murder on the mountain."

Misty's news fell on her like a rock.

"Murder?" Mariah pulled back, her brow furrowed in shock. She knew the word, but hadn't known of it happening in her lifetime. She shook her head. "No, not in Elysium. That couldn't be."

"Fortunately, not in Elysium, this time, but dangerously close. You are needed ..." Misty hesitated. *"The one you seek is found. There is no more time for talk. It is late, and you must go."*

"Now? But I just got here. I'm not expected back for a

while."

"Look, the sun is past the falls—the lights dance no more."

Mariah hadn't noticed. The dancing lights had disappeared from the walls and the cave had darkened from their absence.

"Oh no, Momma will pluck me good if she finds out."

"Windy is delayed. Be strong, Mariah. There are some whom you cannot trust any longer. You will know them by their heart.

"You must go to the Anasazi village. Chief Bending Tree needs you and you are in need of him. Do not be afraid—farewell my young queen."

The puffs of mist disappeared back inside the crack and the crystal lights went out.

"Wait! Don't go. What do I … ?"

Mariah stood alone. A feeling of dread spread through her—*what disaster waits on the other side?*

Her mind numb, she climbed to the upper ledge where the waterfall poured over the cliff, and then she took a brief rest. The falling water would hit hard, so to make sure she broke through she pressed herself far against the back of the cave like she had four years before. The muscles in her arms and legs flexed as she made ready to sprint. A few deep breaths and she sprang forward.

The water hit hard, but her strength and speed pushed her through the other side where she made a clean dive into the lake. Talons grabbed her shoulders as soon as she surfaced and lifted her to the shore.

"Moon, what's the big hurry?"

"Something awful has happened. They're all waiting down below. Come on, we've got to go now."

Mariah didn't say another word; neither did Moon. Events played out beyond her control, as if in a bad dream. Not knowing the horror beyond, she held on to her numbness, thinking it might come in handy.

Somewhere over the rim of Elysium, Feller met up with them. He said nothing, not even a whistle. He simply escorted them to the site.

While they drifted down the ridge and out of Elysium, Mariah saw the gathering of eagles and other animals at the base of the steep terrain. They gathered around a thick, dead tree with most of its branches broken off from time and weather. Directly in front of the tree, Kodiak stood laboring away at something.

When they drew close, the others turned to see Mariah, Moon, and Feller coming. Their faces looked dreadful. With a few backward swoops of her wings, Moonglider landed reverently with the rest. Mariah slid from Moon's back and took a few shaky steps forward. Kodiak stepped aside, swaying her head sadly from side to side, the fur on her neck and shoulders bristled.

Mariah stopped, unable to go further. Her eyes stung with tears of rage and disbelief as she stared woodenly at what every animal had already witnessed. A lump grew so big in her throat that she almost choked. She couldn't believe the atrocity. Flies buzzed everywhere and the air reeked of rot. Her stomach knotted inside making her lightheaded and sick. She fell to her knees and threw up.

The numbness lifted. She didn't want to look again and see the dead stare of the beautiful face. She didn't want to see his fangless mouth matted with blood. She didn't want to see Puma suspended over the ground with his front paws stretched and pinned against the tree by two large boulders. She didn't want to see again the five bloody holes that pierced his heart.

Mariah wished she was back in the cave, safe from the outside world, but she wasn't. Reality was cruel—this was not a good day as she'd thought just a short time ago. A wing embraced her. She looked up into her mother's eyes and could think and breathe again, but only in ragged heaves. Her tear-stained face lifted and a moan swelled in her throat. "Take him down," she wailed. "Please, someone, take him down!"

Windy squeezed Mariah a little tighter. "Kodiak has been trying, my love. She's the strongest one here and hasn't been able to move either stone."

Mariah didn't care; she stood and thrust herself against one of the rocks that held Puma suspended to the old tree. She pushed with all her strength, but the rock wouldn't budge. "Help!" she commanded. "In the name of Misty, help him!"

She felt a certain power suddenly pulse from deep in her emotions. It sizzled out of her hands and into the granite, cracking a few veins through it. She had no idea what it was or how to control it—it simply came and no one noticed.

"Misty?" someone in the crowd said in a harsh voice. "Who else but Misty could have done this?"

Mariah stopped; she couldn't believe what she'd heard. She stepped away from the stone and wiped a tear from her red-streaked face. "Who said that?" she demanded.

With a few swoops of his wings, an eagle bounded over the others and landed in front of her. Windy's brother, Windstorm, stood with a smug look on his face. "Who else commands stones this large to be tossed about?" he sneered. "It's obvious this execution was carried out by Misty's power and authority. Anyone here can plainly see that."

Mariah's emotions were raw—her grief turned to anger. She stormed straight to her uncle and slapped him hard across his dagger-like beak.

Windstorm flashed her a hot glare, the feathers on his neck and head hackled.

"How dare you!" she screamed. "Of all the animals under Misty's care, an eagle should know better. This is not the work of our Mountain and you know it. You ought to be ashamed of yourself to even suggest such a thing."

Kodiak raised herself threateningly on her hind legs and snarled at the bird.

Windstorm moved back.

The bear, seeing she'd made her point, charged instead into the boulder with a new vigor, bouncing her weight hard against the top.

"What are you doing, Storm?" Windy's glare cut deep. "You shouldn't talk about Misty this way, especially in front of the rest. What earthly reason would Misty have to pierce cruel holes in Puma like that? It makes no sense."

"Oh really, now, Windy," Windstorm said, still keeping a leery eye on the bear. "Any beast who craves the dead could have done it, don't you think." His chuckled oozed with sarcasm. "Filthy crows, perhaps? Worms? Who else but our beloved Mountain is able to move stone like that? It would otherwise be impossible." He cast a cold gaze around, then raised his voice. "Evidently, Misty is not whom we all believe him to be!"

Windy lost her calm and her feathers hackled out all over, making her appear larger than she really was. Screaming Eagle flew in between the two, and stopped her from doing something she would regret.

"All right, that's enough! Windstorm, shut your beak and fly on out of here. There'll be no more talk like that about Misty. There's enough trouble here and we don't need you adding to it, or I'll be making trouble of my own. Understood?" The muscles in his jaws flexed.

Windstorm scanned the animals, a seething expression on his face. A few seemed to be thinking on his words, but most gave him little sympathy. Reluctant, he spread his wings and vanished into the summer air.

On the outskirts of the crowd, a wolverine turned and trotted away into the woods, and a badger trailed behind.

"Let them go," Screaming Eagle said. "Windy and Mariah are right, it makes no sense. What has Puma ever done? Even if he did something unforgivable, Misty would never do a thing like this. This is not his doing."

With a snort, a bull moose showed his support by joining Kodiak. He wedged his antler between the boulder and tree, and pried. Others wanted to help too, but would have been hurt in the process. The moose and bear proved to be enough.

From where Mariah had fractured cracks, the stone moved. They pushed harder and the boulder soon split in half, toppled over, and slid down the short incline to the base of the slope.

Like a puppet whose string had just been cut, the dead lion flopped pathetically to the opposite boulder that still trapped his other paw.

Mariah shrieked and turned away. "Please get him down—please!"

The moose and bear made short work of the other boulder. Puma fell to the ground, freed at last of his humiliation.

His burial was swift, but reverent. Wolves prepared a hole in the earth far away from the tree of his execution, where he was laid to rest under the towering shade of his lookout tree in Elysium Valley.

Puma would be forever missed.

Chapter 17
Same Game

Snap—

"Watch yer step, ya lumbering idiot. They can hear us from here, ya know," Erikson whispered sharply.

The men moved with stealth through the dark forest. Just before dawn, the stars still shone as clear pinpoints in the sky. Red lined the eastern rim of the earth as if a knife had slit the morning open.

"Did ya bring the meat likes I told ya?"

"Aye, gots it here, I do." Toby pried a chunk of raw flesh from his front pants pocket and gripped it tight with his bulky fist. Bloody juice dripped between his fingers. "See, Cap, here it be." The dangling meat slapped Erikson in the face.

"Blimey. Fer the love of dung. Put that bloody thing away," he hissed, and pushed Toby's hand back into his face.

Toby's head drew down between his shoulders while Erikson wiped his cheek with the back of his sleeve. The old captain glared at the shadowed outline of his companion with disgust. "Don't be tellin' me ya had that bloody thing in yer pocket all this time?"

"Aye, Cap," he answered, hesitant.

Erikson breathed a heavy, disgusted sigh. "Ya flea-bitten fool. I's told ya ta put it in the bag I gave ya, an' ta strap it to yer belt. Does I have ta watch everything ya do? If'n ya be done squeezin' the life out of it, ya might as well be stickin' it back in yer pocket so's we can be off."

Toby's lower lip pouted below the crooked nose Skye had kicked and broken sixteen years before. Ever since, it wheezed like a snoring moose.

Erikson found Toby's dull looks—accentuated by the warbling noise of his nose—disturbing, and made him breathe through his mouth most of the time. The open jaws didn't help his looks any but kept the hideous sound to a minimum.

"Follow me carefully now, ya hear? An' keep yer bloody, floppin' feet off o' twigs."

"Aye Cap—bless da king." Toby wedged the large chunk of meat back into his front pocket then wiped the blood from his hand under his arm.

"An' don't be startin' blessin' no king with me either—'least not till we gets what's we come fer."

Toby bobbed his head twice.

From tree to tree they plodded on a cushion of pine needles until they reached a clearing in the woods. For the most part they moved silently, but Erikson couldn't always count on silence for proper sneaking. He had to be prepared for the unexpected.

"I's feels it drawin' me, Cap," Toby whispered, bouncing up and down on his toes. "You can feel it too, cain't ya? I 'member it doin'—"

"Quiet. Yer gonna wake the—"

Woof!

A dog's bark broke the sleeping morning. The captain and Toby froze on either side of the tree they were hugging and waited. All seemed quiet, then ...

Snortle–ortle–ortle. Snortle ...

A hideous, soggy, rattling sound reverberated through the cool autumn air.

Snortle–ortle ...

Somewhere on the other side of the darkness, several dog growls answered.

"Toby—" Erikson's sharp whisper cut like broken glass.

Toby dropped his jaw open and slapped a hand over his mouth, just to be sure.

A few more growls and a few more *woofs*, and several dogs came closer to investigate.

"Nows ya done it. Ya might as well have stood up an' shouted 'woopy' fer all the good our sneakin's done."

Toby was too excited to pay attention. "Dogs, Cap! I likes dogs. King's got a dog—bless da King."

Erikson rolled his eyes and sighed. "Aye, Toby, king's—got—a—dog," he whispered. "Now if'n ya don't mind, nows be a good time ta be takin' the meat from yer pocket an' quietin' the bloody beasts ya jus' done disturbed before they wakes the whole village."

Toby yanked the raw meat from his blood-soaked trousers. "Can I pets 'em too, Cap? I loves pettin' 'em."

The captain resigned himself. "Aye, Toby. Fer that matter, I insist. Love the bloody weasels all ya wants, jus' don't say nothin'. An' keep yer mouth open, 'kay, lad?"

Despite Toby being forty years old, the aging captain, now in his seventies, still referred to his simpleminded companion as 'lad' if he wasn't referring to him as something else of a more derogatory nature.

Toby fell to his knees and coaxed the dogs, using the meat to befriend them. Before long, six tail-wagging, tongue-licking canines surrounded them, eating out of Toby's hands.

The stocky oaf had a way with animals that the captain didn't understand, but he made sure he petted the dogs himself so they would be acquainted with him as well.

After a few minutes, a faint blush lit the sky, sending tree shadows into the center of the village.

Erikson leaned over to where Toby sat with his arms around the shoulders of two dogs, hugging them close. "Best be movin' on now, lad," he whispered into his ear.

A worried look crossed Toby's face. He fixed the Captain with sad eyes and tugged his coat, dragging Erikson down with it. He whispered, jabbing a thick finger at the dogs who were contentedly tearing at their breakfast. "But theys ain't done yet, Cap."

"It be all right, Toby." He gave a reassuring pat. "We's planned it that way, 'member? They stays here an' eats whiles we goes in there ... an' takes." He pointed across the court to where a larger hut could just be made out in the early dawn.

Toby sat there, eyes pleading with the captain.

Erikson cleared his throat and put a knee down beside Toby and the dogs. When Toby was like this he had to change tactics. "Aye, mighty fine beasts, they be," he whispered, stroking a dog's ear. "Ya gots a good eye fer beauty, ya do, Toby, me lad. I be wantin' to stay with 'em, as well. Can hardly tear meself away, if'n I be tellin' the truth."

Sometimes manipulation worked better on Toby than a whip, especially when they needed stealth. He leaned over and whispered into Toby's ear. "I's heard it too, mate. I's feel it drawin' me likes ya told me it be doin' you, 'member?"

Toby's eyes hardened with purpose again. "Aye, Cap, I's 'member. Drawin' me like a fly, 'twas."

Erikson stood up and extended a hand. "It's time, matey. Destiny calls."

"Destiny calls, bless da king." Toby took hold of the captain's hand.

"Aye, bless the king, indeed." Erikson pulled Toby to his feet, squeezing his shoulder with the other hand. "Ya makes me proud, laddie."

Toby breathed in deeply and puffed out a proud chest. *Snortle—ortle*

Erikson shook his head in surrender, pushed a finger down on Toby's chin, then swept a skinny hand before him. "After ya, mate ... quietly this time, if'n ya don't mind."

Toby gave a quick rub to each of the dogs before stooping over with Erikson's guiding hand on his back. They moved quietly across the court to the hogan they'd once known as the Hut of Peace. One quick look around the dimly-lit village and they slipped through the thick rug door undetected, just as planned.

When they looked around the glowing room, and breathed in spiced air, they knew they had finally made it back. They stood mesmerized, looking at the compelling stone as it glowed in its own light—the treasure in all its glory—wasting away in a display room for unworthy savages.

After sixteen years of fearing the mountain—sixteen miserable years eking out a thieving living and reliving, over and over, that one brief moment with Bending Tree and the stone—they finally worked up enough nerve to come back. Erikson wondered if the mountain would spit fire and try to swallow them again. He didn't care anymore. At his age it was worth the risk before death caught up with him. His lust for life and wealth drove him to get the stone, or die trying. He'd convinced himself this would be his last chance for eternal youth, and he would take that chance.

He felt fairly sure that he and Toby were the only ones outside the village who knew of the stone, and there it sat, lustrous and still cradled in its place of honor, waiting for him. The stone purred and its turquoise light illuminated the room.

"Look at the lights, Cap. Be it alive?" Toby bounced up and down on his toes again, his eyes as big as pinecones.

"Aye, that it be, Toby, me boy. Makes a man wonder if what they says about it be true." He put his hand near the stone and felt the warmth of the pulsating oracle. His heart leapt. Both men took a deep breath of the enveloping peace and, together, exhaled.

"Makes me mind feel like I's jus' took a nap, Cap."

"Ah, the scent of this place invigorates me bones too, laddie. If that be its virtue, then we's gonna be a happy pair, Toby, me boy. After all these years, finally rich an' happy—an' young."

The throbbing light dazzled their eyes to an unblinking stare; greed blocking everything else out. Erikson had found what so many others still sought, and to possess it would bring him all he wanted—his genie in a bottle, a slave to his bidding.

"Gots ta have it, mate," Erikson whispered, his eyes still fixed on the stone. His lower lip trembled with the adrenalin surging through his veins.

"Gots ta have it, mate," Toby echoed without blinking.

"It be drawin' me like a flyyy." The captain stared as if hypnotized.

"Likes a *bloody—buuzzin'—flyyyy ...*" Toby said.

The room lit up with early morning sun. With a grunt, the captain tore his gaze from the stone and turned to see the faces of Bending Tree and Yenene. Erikson bared his yellow teeth; an unnatural *hiss* wheezed from his throat. He turned back and lunged for the stone, knocking the stand over in the process. "I've gots it!" he shouted. "I've gots it, Toby—run!"

Toby didn't hesitate. After sixteen years of thieving together, the captain knew Toby would react at a moment's notice. He plowed through the doorway with his thick body and strong legs, taking the older leader and medicine man with him. They tumbled to the ground in a disheveled heap of arms and legs. Erikson escaped through the doorway, but purposely stopped long enough to plant a foot into the side of the chief before he ran woodenly from the village, cradling the stone like a baby.

He knocked two women aside, scattering their morning meals to the ground as he fled. Toby hastily picked himself up and, imitating the captain, kicked the chief before bumbling after Erikson. He followed close behind, tromping through the debris while dogs jumped around him, wanting in on the game.

"Toby!" the captain screamed, plodding along with his prize.

"Comin', Cap!"

"Remember, we's don't needs the mule no more. Jus' get me musket an' meets me over wheres we planned—across the river at the large rock wheres the red bush grows. Musket—large rock—bush. Now get yer bloody bones a movin' before they's all come a huntin' us."

"Aye, Cap." He paused to pet a dog then detoured to

where they'd tethered the pack mule. "Musket—rock—bush," he repeated as he continued his mission. "Musket—rock—bush."

The day before, Erikson had found a shallow spot in the river where the water ran waist deep. He planned his escape by crossing here then crossing it again farther down, where he'd tied his horse. He'd designed the plan to throw pursuers off his trail, and maybe this time in his final escape, leave Toby behind.

After sixteen long years, Toby had worn on the captain. Now that he had the fountain of youth, he didn't want to spend eternity lugging around a halfwit. He wanted a new life and new companions, women—lots of them. Yes, Toby would have to stay behind. His last useful task would be to slow the people down by getting captured. Erikson smiled at his thoroughness.

He moved stealthily, not believing he finally held what he had waited over sixteen years to possess. Images of wealth and life beyond age danced through his imagination as he carried the stone through the forest. A wave of giddiness washed over him.

"I've gots it, by God. It's mine—hee-hee-hee. They said it couldn't be found. Said it couldn't be taken. Said it didn't exist. Those fools. It was so simple—hee-hee. So easy, hee-hee-hee ..."

Erikson stopped abruptly at the river's edge and bobbed his head about, searching. His smile faded into a frown. "Where's that blundering oaf? Those savages oughts ta be on our tails any moment an' I's gots ta have me musket. Toby!" A hint of panic colored his voice. "Blast him anyway!"

Erikson didn't wait; he had to trust that Toby wouldn't forget anything or lose his way. He started across the river, but in his haste slipped and fell splashing into the water. After a moment of flailing, he righted himself, still clutching the living-stone with one arm and gripping a rock from the river bottom with his free hand. In his anger, he almost threw the rock away, but it gleamed bright through his fingers in the morning sun.

"Hello, what's we gots here?" He examined the object then bit into it. "Blimey, well would ya look at that. This 'ere mountain's gots more ta offer than livin'-stones, it do."

The sun, still struggling to rise above the trees, cast shafts of light through the branches and over the river where a golden radiance reflected from the bottom. Erikson brushed his hand a few times over the waters as if trying to clear the ripples. "Well, bless the king. The whole bloody river's lined with 'em. Heee–heee."

He inhaled to yell again for Toby, but caught the word before letting it fly. He looked around suspiciously to see if anyone was watching, then crossed the river quickly, sloshed over to a nearby boulder, and hunched behind it, dripping wet. He caught his breath and watched for Toby and any pursuers from the village.

The captain just about burst with excitement; this was the best break he'd ever had in life—gold and the fountain of youth all in one day. He couldn't take the gold with him just yet, but he had a plan.

"First we's takes care o' the stone," he told himself, "then when things settles down a bit, an' I gets back me youth, I can sneaks me way back an' 'ave 'er all to meself. Spring be best at earliest. Aye, waitin' till spring it is." His grin stretched wide at the thought, then he screamed. "*Toby!* Blast the halfwit." He rubbed his cold fingers over the warm, humming surface of the stone. "Probably stopped to play with the bloody beasts." Then he mocked Toby with his face skewed, "King's got a dog—King's got a dog! Heee–heee." He said it again just for fun. "King's got a dog!"

Still chuckling, Erikson cradled his trophy and trudged on in the direction of the rock by the red bush. He still had a ways to go, and his wet clothes made traveling more difficult.

With each step away from the village, the oracle increased its sound. The humming became a whine and then a shriek, and an unpleasant scent oozed from its pores. It became much too warm and began to gyrate in his hands. The farther he went, the louder it screamed and the more violently it shook.

The vibration became so severe that his hands and upper arms tingled with numbness. It bruised his chest and the sound became deafening. Still, determined to have his prize, Erikson clung to the living-stone like a drowning man clings to a life preserver.

The stench and siren of the stone became so appalling that Erikson's sinuses and inner ears pounded in pain. He became nauseated to the point of vomiting and stopped to do just that. Undeterred, he clutched as best he could to the oracle and trudged onward. He would never willingly release the treasure that promised eternal youth and riches.

Before crossing the river, he'd thought possessing the stone was a pleasant dream, but now he wondered if the dream hadn't turned into a nightmare.

When he reached the top of the hill, he could see the bright red bush in the autumn sunlight. He'd almost made it. But the stone got increasingly hot, and Erikson lost control of his overtaxed limbs. The stone tumbled to the ground, where it continued to rattle and scream louder and louder. He could do no more; his arms had become limp, totally useless.

He whimpered in pain, grieving his loss, and rocked his head from shoulder to shoulder trying to block the hideous sound. Not wanting to leave it behind, he knelt and commanded his limbs to grasp it, but they wouldn't comply. Again he tried—nothing. He couldn't even lift his arms to cover his ears. The pain felt maddening and the ringing in his head drove him crazy.

He staggered to his feet and ran, tripping blindly about the trees and rocks while his arms flopped lifelessly at his sides. He had to get away … had to leave the treasured stone with the mountain. He didn't care anymore. He hated the stone, he hated the mountain, and he was glad to be rid of them both. He hummed loudly to himself as he ran, trying to drown out the tormenting siren in his head, to no avail.

He was losing his mind.

Not far from the hill, with a single backpack and musket in hand, Toby intercepted the captain.

"Cap," he yelled, "wait up!"

He ran after him and caught him by the shoulders. "What's be wrong, Cap? Is they comin' fer us? I's gots da musket."

Erikson hunched his shoulders and tilted his head from one side to the other, trying to reach his ears as if they itched. Sweat dripped from his head and scraggly beard.

Toby felt confused at the captain's strange behavior. He wanted it to stop. He sniffed the putrid scent, and it made even his deformed nose wrinkle. "What's be wrong, Cap?" he whined. "Stop bein' wrong. I came jus' likes ya told me. See, gots yer musket, I do. You can stop now."

"Wants the treasure. Needs the treasure. But I can'ts have it," the captain said through sobs. "Why can'ts I have it? I need it, wants it. It be mine now, but I can'ts have it."

Toby blinked, feeling a little scared. He'd never seen the captain cry. To him, Erikson was the toughest, bravest, wisest man he knew. "Where be da stone, Cap? What's ya done with it?"

"It don't want me," Erikson whined. "Don'ts like me. Attack me, it did." He threw his head in the direction of the sound and spat. "Blast ya cursed, bouncing, babbling, bloody stone of insanity." he screamed. "Curse ya, I say. Curse ya bloody promises an' curse the mountain." He spat again before folding to the ground in a miserable, sobbing heap.

A polluted flame flared in a hollow cavity, sending a puff of yellow smoke twirling past silver lips. On a hill against the rocky slope of Misty's timberline, overlooking the men, a hooded figure watched with large, silver eyes. Its mouth arched beautifully, an endorsement of the hateful cursing. The creature was pleased.

Erikson would do nicely.

Chapter 18
The Big Bang

"Who's a Momma's girl now?" Mariah stuck a playful tongue out at Moonglider.

"Oh, stop rubbing it in," Moon grumbled. "The day's ruined enough as it is." She looked up with pleading eyes to her mother who came to see Windy and Mariah off. *"Mo-om?"* she begged once more.

"Moon," Moonbeam cautioned her daughter. "We've already discussed this, dear. Misty called Mariah, not you. He knows what he's doing. This is her time to go, and it's only right that her mother should take her. It is the man village, you know, not the lake. And the Mountain knows you get in enough trouble as it is down there." Moonbeam ruffled her daughter's feathered head with her wing. "I'm sure someday, if you're still willing, Misty will call you too."

Moon tried ducking out from under the ruffling without looking too disrespectful. "This isn't going to be any fun," she muttered.

For Moon, the day was over, the morning sun might

as well be setting. To stay at home would be unbearably dull for her. Mariah came over and consoled her, tapping her on the wing with the back of her hand. "It's okay, Moon, I'll tell you all about it when we come back. And I promise to bring you something, too."

"Really? Like what?"

A mischievous gleam came to Mariah's face. "Like an armful of berries." She chuckled.

"Oh, yuck. Berries?" Moon gagged. "Berries are for crows an' bears an' squirrels ..."

"An' little girls," Mariah said.

"Yes, and little girls. I'd rather eat a skunk."

"Skunk it is." Mariah said. "Come on, Mom, we better go before Moon changes her mind. Quick." Mariah pushed her mother playfully.

Windy and Moonbeam laughed at their daughters.

"Not so quick. You didn't ask if she wanted a one or two-striped skunk. There's a difference, you know," Windy said with a wink.

"Don't know, Ma. Don't think she'd care—she loves 'em both. We'll bring back one of each and let her decide."

"Yeah, and you can eat the other," Moon shot back. "Remember what Screaming Eagle always tells you—waste not, want not."

"Believe me, Moon, if you can eat a skunk so can I. Deal?"

"Deal!"

Mariah's smile lessened as she put an arm around Moon's neck. "I'm gonna miss you, too, Moon."

"How long are you going to be gone?"

"Don't really know. A couple days of or so; hopefully no more."

"Are you scared? I know I would be."

"Yeah, a little. More nervous than anything, I guess. I'd rather not go, but Misty made it sound real important. Don't even know what to do when I get there."

"You think they'll know our language? 'Cause we certainly can't understand their gibberish."

"That troubles me the most. What am I gonna do if they don't?"

"Well, you can always do what Feller does and whistle lots."

"Yeah." She chuckled. "We'll just sit there whistling and chirping at each other. Who knows, maybe we'll come up with a song for you about snackin' on skunks!"

That morning, like most autumn mornings, the valley lay sunny and warm with a tinge of crispness to the air. The forest, spotted with brilliant yellow aspens and red oak brush, stood out dramatically against the green of the pines.

Excited and nervous for their mother-daughter adventure, Windy and Mariah drifted on a meandering flight toward the base of the mountain where the river spilled from the lake. There really wasn't any hurry and a leisurely journey would help settle their nerves before they landed unannounced in the middle of the village.

From Elysium's upper ridge, where he hunted for seasonal flowers, Feller caught sight of them soaring over the lake. He forgot the flowers and made a straight line to intercept them, whistling as he went. With Windy's speed, it would take some effort to meet up with them.

Feller hadn't seen Mariah fly with her mother very often. Usually she flew with Moon, but here they were, headed straight into the fog of the eastern ridge. In a few minutes, they would plunge through. He put more fluttering power into his wings and, as he got closer, he saw their expressions were neither happy nor sad ... more determined than anything. Not at all like Mariah, who would typically be making some kind of jubilant noise. He wanted to see what they were up to before the clouds swallowed them up.

Windy called out before plunging into the clouds— something the eagles always did to avoid colliding with another eagle or bird.

"Wahooo!" Mariah followed with her signature cry and disappeared into the mist.

Now that's more like Mariah, thought Feller as he disappeared in Misty's foggy soup, chirping as he followed.

The exuberant shout echoed down the rocky head of Misty and reached the guardian's ears.

"Now where have I heard that before?" Igneous said. He rolled along the tunnels and up to the mouth of Misty where he peered down into the bubbling eye. "Hey, Misty, let's have a look, why don't we?"

Misty's eye closed and disappeared below the gurgling surface. A white haze meshed on the churning lava where the eye had been floating. An image tried to materialize out of the filmy white.

Igneous tapped his stony finger against the ledge. "Come on, come on, I'm not getting any younger, you know. Hmm, come to think of it, I'm not getting any older either."

He cleared his throat and struck up a pose. "Come

now, thy luminous mountain, I implore thee, illuminate yonder outside world so thou and I may gaze upon thither joyous shouts."

"Igneous, my dear Shakespearian guardian, the two are flying through clouds at this moment. I'm sure they'll be coming out soon," Misty gurgled.

"Oh yeah, I knew that, never mind. Sorry. We never got to foresee this part before, and I'm curious how they're going to meet and all that formal stuff. It's always exciting watching first-time friendships, don't you think?

"Hey, you suppose she'll fall in love? I've been noticing Pony eyeing her when she flies near the village. I say they'll have their first kiss before the next full moon. What do you think? … Oh no," Igneous continued before Misty could answer. "If she falls in love, how is she ever going to want to leave? Huh? Ever think of that? Great balls of lava. Who didn't think this whole idea through anyway? You know, haste is not so—"

KA—BANG!

A thunderous sound exploded through the cavern and the mountain trembled.

Misty's eye came quickly to the surface. "Igneous! Igneous, what happened?"

Igneous clutched his chest as if he had been shot through the heart. His face gnarled with pain and an eagle's shriek screamed from his throat. The cloudy image on the surface of Misty's eye showed a tumbling mass of feathers mixed in swirling fog. Both Mariah and Windy tumbled and fell in an endless sea of white.

At the same time that late morning, on a different part

of the mountain, Bending Tree stood on a boulder. He gazed across the slopes that led to the mountain and listened to the air, his silver-streaked hair lifting in the breeze.

Pony and Honovi waited below for the chief. They watched an eagle high on the mountain above Misty's clouds carrying something on its back. The sound of Bending Tree jumping from the rock startled the men.

"It is time," said Bending Tree. "I hear the stone calling to us from those slopes, there." He pointed to several large boulders across the river toward the top of a hill. "We must go."

The young men tried to keep up with the old man who paced swiftly toward the screaming stone. They crossed the river and continued up the rocky slopes. The sound increased as they approached.

"There." said Pony. "Is that it, Father?"

A satisfied smile came to the old chief's face. "I believe so. Look, it jumps with joy at our presence."

They quickened their pace. The stone sensed their presence when they drew near and its gyrating deflated to the calming throb of a heartbeat. The putrid scent reverted to the spicy aroma.

Bending Tree lifted the stone in cupped hands. The boys gathered around it, each putting a hand to its warm surface and breathing its healing scent. Like a kitten after mealtime, it purred.

Bending Tree lifted the stone to the mountain in thanksgiving. As he prepared to speak, the stone pulsed a single burst of light against his hands and up though his arms. He jolted with the impact and for a moment his face looked radiant, and tears of joy ran down his cheeks. He opened his mouth and let the stone speak through him:

> *"Come to me, my child,*
> *and let me heal your soul.*
> *Peace of mind and body be yours,*
> *if that truly be your goal.*
> *But let not lust nor passions be*
> *your guide that begs through greed.*
> *For whatever your heart's desire,*
> *truly you shall receive."*

Bending Tree saw the look of confusion on the boys' faces. He lowered the stone, and looked calmly at them. "Do not be afraid, the stone knows us." His eyes flicked to the breathing oracle in his hands. "It senses our emotions. It senses the good in us—and senses the bad. Good heart—good help from the stone. Bad heart—beware." He pulled his brows together in a piercing look, then relaxed. The corners of his mouth curved up. He put a hand on the nape of Pony's neck, looking at him then Honovi. A smile flickered in his eyes. "Do not ever be afraid of the stone, my young men. The stone knows your heart and it is pleased."

"Look." Honovi pointed to the sky. "Above the clouds, there, the eagle girl rides."

They looked to the sky and beheld the beauty and grace of her flight.

"She's coming this way." Pony said.

The eagle and girl plunged into the vastness of the clouds, and disappeared. From inside the clouds, faint but clear, came a joyous shout:

"Wahooo!"

"You are right, Honovi." Bending Tree smiled. "It is nice to hear it ring through the valle—"

KA—BANG!

The mountain quaked and the trees quivered as if a

gust of wind had struck them. The stone jumped in Bending Tree's hands then whined mournfully. All around the mountain, eagles flew from their nests and filled the air.

Again, at that moment, at a higher elevation on the mountain, a bleak mist surrounded the two men. Light reflected off velvet drops of moisture, giving their surroundings an eerie cast.

Erikson lay shivering by a smoldering fire somewhere between sleep and consciousness. Toby sat with his back against a rock, darting both his gaze and his head about like a falcon in a room full of rats. He clutched the loaded musket and wrung it with twitching fingers.

"They be comin', Cap," Toby whispered. "I can feels it in me bones. Sneakin', they be, from below. Waitin' 'til we drops dead in the cold, I warrant." He shivered and pulled his coat tighter around himself. "Gots to get away from the bloody forest, we do."

Toby slipped his hand under Erikson's arm and helped him to his feet. "They's be comin' fer us, Cap. Gots ta get away now." His voice grew frantic.

They stumbled over rocks to higher ground. Though the climb became difficult, the movement brought warmth to their bodies. But ghosts still muddled their minds. A rock dislodged beneath their feet, and fell, skipping down over boulders.

"What be that?" Erikson spoke for the first time since that morning. His red eyes went wild with panic, and his breathing grew heavier. "Toby!" He turned, trying to clutch at Toby's sleeve. "What be that? Does ya see them, Toby? Toby!"

"I, I don't know Cap. I can't see a bloody thing through da fog. Theys be following us, all right. Gonna attack, they be." He tugged at the captain's sleeve. "Come, Cap, gots ta keep movin'."

Somewhere in the distance, the cry of an eagle shattered the thick clouds, and what sounded like a human voice gave a battle cry:

"Wahooo!"

It echoed through the canyon, but the men didn't know from what direction it came. Toby thrust the musket to his shoulder, and turned in all directions, expecting an attack from the natives at any moment.

"They're comin' fer us Cap. They're comin'." Toby's panicked voice sent a noticeable shiver through the captain. "Run fer it!"

Erikson trotted blindly through the fog, his lifeless arms dangling in front of him while he tripped over rocks and bumped into boulders.

With a grunt, Toby jerked the musket into the air as a large dark image barreled through the fog. He pulled the trigger.

KA—BANG!

Chapter 19
Scram

"Eeeaacck!"

A single musket ball drilled deep into Windy's heart. Blood ran as she plummeted, screaming, to the rocks below.

Feller stopped in midair when he heard the blast. He didn't flee like most birds would have done—he studied the situation. Through the last echoes of the explosion came descending screams from the sky, cut off by hollow sounds hitting cold stone. He went to investigate, zipping here and there, but couldn't see a thing in the milky atmosphere.

He whistled.

No answer.

He chirped.

Silence.

Through the haunting mists, sounds of voices reverberated in the fog. Feller cautiously sped toward the racket, thinking it might be Windy and Mariah hiding from the noise. He whistled sprightly as if to say, *Here I am*, but he didn't find what he expected. Never had he seen men like these. They staggered and stumbled, hurrying away from something. For the next few minutes, Feller forgot his original pursuit and fluttered to the thin man, stopping inches from his face. He wasn't pleased to see them sneaking about and wanted to know what they were doing on his mountain.

"Chirp, squeak–chirp, chirp!" he challenged with all the authority of a courageous hummingbird.

Erikson flinched, then swatted at the object before him.

Toby turned and saw him flailing his arms.

"Get away from me, ya little demon!" the captain yell to an unseen attacker.

Toby thought the captain had finally lost his mind and was slapping at ghosts. He spooked easily enough as it was, and thought about leaving the captain behind and coming back for him later. Then he saw what looked like a floating rock dashing in and around Erikson's thrashing arms. It eased his mind to know the captain was actually swatting at something real.

"Toobyy!" Erikson shrieked for help, then cried pitifully, *"To-ho-byy!"*

Toby jammed the musket against his shoulder and followed the hovering object around Erikson's head. He arched his bushy eyebrows, puffed his cheeks full of air, and held his breath to steady his aim. While Erikson swatted empty air, Toby followed the object in his sights. He didn't consider how dangerously close his shot would be to taking Erikson's head off or how hard it would be to hit a small darting object.

"Too-hoo-byyy!"

Toby puffed his cheeks up again with fresh air. Ready or not, he took aim and squeezed the trigger.

Click

Toby cursed the misfire and quickly pulled the hammer back. Again, he filled his cheeks and took aim.

Click

Toby then realized he'd forgotten to reload the firearm after the last shot.

"Comin', Cap." He grabbed the musket by the barrel like a club and swung it, slicing the fog in an arc. He swung again at the flying object, missed, and shattered the musket handle against a boulder. With determined fury, he repeatedly jabbed the broken musket at the dodging bird, missing and jabbing until finally he connected … with the captain's jaw.

Erikson hit the ground hard, a bloody spot gaping where a few teeth once had been. On the ground, he groped the cold earth with one hand and mechanically swatted a few more times with the other before passing out.

Toby didn't realize he'd struck the very person he'd set out to protect. He swung and yelled, cursed and stabbed, but the hummingbird was quick.

In a flurry of whistles and wings, it fought back, ramming its beak into the side of Toby's face, piercing his cheeks over and over again.

Toby dropped the broken musket and palmed each of his bleeding cheeks. Tears sprang to his eyes and he sobbed, snorting heaves of terror. He'd never liked the mountain anyway, and only came because Erikson said so.

All around them, snapping and twisting granite groaned from deep within the earth. The large boulders that surrounded the area quivered with increasing violence, and sent rocks skipping down the steep embankment. Toby stumbled to his knees when rocks buffeted him, and tore his clothes and skin. He fell to the ground beside the captain, clutching him. "Cap." He shook the limp body while stones crashed around him. "I wants ta go now, Cap. Caaap? I wants ta go!"

He patted Erikson's ashen face and felt a familiar sticky mess. He smeared a red stubby thumb against his fingers and panicked. "Cap? Don't go, Cap. I don't know whats ta do," he whined amid the bombarding rocks.

Deep beneath the earth, granite popped and split, sending a shockwave of horror through Toby. He hadn't experienced such terror since the mountain tried to swallow him and the captain years ago in pits of fire. But this was worse; he didn't have the captain to tell him what to do. He grabbed Erikson by the front of the jacket and dragged him a few feet, before the falling rocks proved too much for him.

Toby threw his arms over his bald head. His eyes darted over the captain's body. The dust and rubble of the mountain slowly buried him, and he could do nothing about it. Exhausted, wounded, and paralyzed with fear, he wanted out—*now*.

He brushed the dust from Erikson's lifeless face. "Sorry, Cap, sorry," he sobbed. "I's gots ta go now, sorry."

Toby stood on the trembling earth and ran aimlessly through clouds of dust, hands outstretched, leaving his only friend to die on the mountain.

"Sorry!" he shouted back as he tromped through the fog and debris. "Sorry."

He fled the quaking mountain while the tiny bird continued to prod the back of his head.

The fog grew thick and Misty gave a geologic shiver. The quake shook Toby from his feet and shot him down an embankment, where he tumbled with the flow of dislodged rocks and boulders.

The hummingbird paced Toby from the air, watching as he bounced along until he sailed, screaming, off a cliff and disappeared into the fog.

The quaking stopped abruptly and all went quiet—the stillness broken only by a remnant of dislodged stones coming to rest.

Back up the slope, a gem-coated hand of exquisite workmanship thrust down into the debris and took the captain by the throat. After a steady, even pull, Erikson's body lay sprawled atop the pile. Silver fingernails raked slowly down his neck, past his collarbone, and stopped. Slender, jeweled fingers circled over his heart and pushed in. Flesh flamed as the fingers slipped deeper and deeper, past the knuckles, until its palm rested against the man's lifeless chest.

Erikson's eyes flew open. A deep, wheezing breath inhaled past his gaping mouth. Unimaginable pain caught in his throat. He shivered all over, but uttered not a sound; his scream silent.

Beautiful eyes of pure silver stared back at him, and saw into his soul. The captain sensed the creature searching and probing his every impure thought. He felt violated but could do nothing to stop the intrusion.

The creature's silver lips parted and yellow smoke swirled out. It tilted its head back on its shoulders and let out a deep, satisfied sigh. For a moment, its head rocked side to side then fell forward. It opened its penetrating eyes and stared into Erikson's face.

"Do you wish to live?"

The words, smooth as liquid silver, flowed from its perfect mouth in melodic tones.

Erikson's eyes dripped sweet tears at the sound of its voice. He thought nothing of the pain anymore, nor the violation of his thoughts. He felt nothing, desired nothing—except the symphonic flow of music from the creature.

"Do you wish to live?

"You must decide.

"Do I take or give."

It sang its invitation in rhyme like an opera singer.

Erikson's mind melded with the perfect voice and he felt compelled to pull himself up by the arm that held its fingers to his heart. He looked passionately into the silver eyes. A mirror image of himself reflected back. With a weak nod, Erikson mouthed, "Yes."

"I am pleased."

It sang its soothing approval in a whisper.

"It is good to be pleased, is it not true?"

Its fingers squeezed gently against his heart. The captain drank in every lovely tone from its silver tongue and nodded again.

"Ahhh, you do wish to please me then, don't you?"

Silvery harmonics ran sweet with the stench of its fetid breath.

Again the captain nodded, still unable to speak.

"Go to Pandemonium, Erikson.

"Pandemonium brings me pleasure."

Without another word, a quick shot of colored light burst down the creature's arm and into Erikson's chest.

The silent blast dislodged the creature's fingers, and threw the captain back into the pile of dust and stone.

He lay stunned, afraid to touch his seared chest. In his stupor, he heard the wretched cry of an eagle and the flapping of giant wings. Weak, he lifted his head and saw a large dark object fly away with a rider through the dense fog.

He laid his head back down; the creature had gone. Erikson lay alone in the foggy world. Tears dripped down his cheeks, aroused by the purity of the creature's voice. He pulled the singed clothing away from his burning chest. The pain lessened with each ragged breath.

He took his time to sit up, and stared about the misty clouds as if woken from a dream. Despite the memory of the melodious voice ringing sweet in his ears, the screams of the stone still reverberated in his mind. He put his head in his hands and hummed to himself, trying to quiet the screaming while he begged the memory of the angelic voice to overpower it.

"Pandemonium," he said. Erikson stood and spoke the word again. He looked about into the murky air then wandered unsteadily through the foggy maze of boulders. He gave no thought to his missing companion; Toby didn't matter anymore, only the command of the minstrel.

"Pandemonium," he said again, and slowly made his way off the mountain.

Chapter 20
Eulogy

With all the speed he could muster, Misty lifted the fog from the slopes. Gleams of warm sunshine pierced the hurrying clouds, causing wisps of fog to dance on heated rocks.

Far below, lay the half-buried body of the foreigner pinned beneath the rubble. Scavenging birds already circled above.

As if woken from sleep, the hummer remembered. Straight into the air he zipped then halted. Nowhere could he see Mariah or Windy. He whistled a question, but no answer came.

A curious sound found his tiny ears from across the slope where the boulders stood thick on the steep mountainside. Wise to Mariah's tricks, Feller darted away, flying low around a rock to surprise them. Right as he was about to startle them with a whistle, he stopped in midair. Deep within the rocky earth, Misty gave a low rumble at what they both witnessed.

There Mariah and Windy lay, but not how he expected. Feathers peppered the terrain. In the midst of a graveyard of giant stones, Mariah lay across her mother's lifeless body. She cried the cry of eagles in mournful distress, overwhelmed by heaving sobs.

Feller swallowed a feeble chirp that sounded like a question which didn't want to hear the answer. He circled Mariah's head and licked at her ears, but Mariah took no notice.

His little head twisted from side to side. He saw Windy sleeping and gave a whistle, but Windy didn't wake.

He dropped to the ground and felt something sticky under his feet. In a flurry he shot back above the cold earth with blood dripping from his feet.

Ever since Puma's execution, the clouded stare of the deceased had become familiar to Feller. The hummingbird's heart beat wildly—Mariah and Windy weren't playing. Whatever had happened, it was far too serious for him to handle alone. The overwhelming tragedy finally sank in.

Mariah's hair hung to the ground in bloody snarls over her mother's wing. Panic gripped Feller and he pulled her hair until she stirred. She arched herself weakly to one side and tried to focus through the tangled strands of hair. Her left arm hung at an unnatural angle. A bone above her elbow protruded through bleeding flesh. She shifted her weight and reached for him with her good arm.

"Momma won't move, Feller," she whispered, "won't speak—won't play. Go find help, Feller. Go …" Mariah's eyes rolled back into her head and she collapsed against Windy.

Feller jerked into the air. He couldn't believe another

tragedy had come. He shot out into the open sky and sped to the high cliffs of Elysium Valley.

"Igneous! Igneous, are you all right?"

Igneous rested against the cavern, dazed. His glow pulsed weakly, his mouth hung open and his eyes were a puddle of turquoise. "She's gone, isn't she?" he said finally, and rubbed a nervous hand over a protruding crystal in the wall.

"Yes, my old friend … she's gone."

"I felt it, Misty, I felt it deep inside. It was horrible. Such a sad, sad tragedy."

"I know," Misty gurgled. "I felt it too, but in a different way. I have tasted rage and death again upon our mountain, and I fear it is only the beginning. I will need your strength and wisdom to help me. It would be very difficult without you."

"I'll miss her," mumbled the guardian. "I'll miss her compassion for the weak and the strength of her convictions. I'll miss her spirit and beauty that once graced our skies. I'll miss her so much … so much." He couldn't hold back any longer and broke down into tears.

Misty let him sit for awhile in sorrow. His heart broke knowing Windy had gone, and seeing Igneous in such grief.

Eventually, Igneous wiped his stony nose and inhaled raggedly, trying to collect his composure. "Will there be help for the girl?"

"The eagles have been informed by the little one. They're gathering now."

"Give me a little time, if you would? I must go and make preparations for Windy."

Misty understood his need for closure and let him go.

Slowly, the guardian of the mountain rolled down the halls of crystals and gold, humming dirges of long ago. Misty watched with sympathy as he disappeared around a corner, dragging long shadows behind.

"The eagles are coming!" the children announced, pointing and jumping in excitement. In the distance, a dozen or more eagles flew in a V formation of weaving wings. The two in front carried the eagle girl between them.

When the eagles reached the trees beyond the river, the children waved to the sky and ran towards them in excitement, chanting their child's rhyme over and over again:

"Eagle Girl, Eagle Girl, soaring way up high
Come play with me, it's fun, you'll see
Then teach me how to fly!"

The girl didn't answer, nor did she wave like she had in the past. The two eagles clutched her in their talons and her long hair whipped around her limp head.

People rushed from their huts and stopped work to see what new horror approached. Dark cries filled the sky and large, sporadic shadows circled the ground.

Are we under attack? they wondered.

The people found the sheer size and number of their mighty neighbors overwhelming. On several isolated occasions, an eagle or two had come to their aid and, once, two of them had followed Skye when he dropped in from a floating bubble years before. But never in the history of the mountain had such a serious gathering occurred.

The eagles circled once around the village then took positions on the ground. Some remained poised in the sky.

The lead eagle with the girl called several clear warning cries then laid her in the center of the camp. He placed a protective leg across her body and arched his massive wings around her. The bird scanned the area with a threatening eye laced with confusion and anger. The people didn't know whether the eagle wanted to strike out at someone or beg for help, but there he stood until someone figured it out and made the first move.

In opposing lines, the people and eagles faced each other, the limp body of the eagle-girl between. Neither knew what the other would do.

Yenene approached the giant bird. It took everything inside of him to keep from showing fear. To be in the presence of a normal-sized eagle was intimidating enough, but the presence of these giants made for a frightening experience. The birds looked him straight in the eye, and the point of their beaks and dagger-like talons could make short work of him or any other opposing creature. The blood drained from his face, but after looking the eagles over, Yenene realized they were as frightened as he. Yet somehow that didn't comfort him much.

On faith, he approached the great sentinel. With hands raised, he went down on one knee, turned his palms up, and dropped his arms until they pointed to the injured girl beneath the bird. The eagle watched every move carefully.

"Brother Eagle," Yenene greeted him in the formal way. They couldn't understand him any more than he could decipher the squawks and shrieks of their language, but it made him feel better to verbalize his thoughts. "We mean no harm to you, or your daughter of the sky. You are welcome here. Your daughter is hurt. We can help."

Yenene sent some women for blankets and hot water then approached the broken girl. When he came closer, the eagle cautiously folded his wings back and pulled his leg from over the girl.

Yenene looked upon the girl and wondered at her story. He reached over and placed a hand to her head.

"She's cold and has lost much blood," he said, looking up into worried eyes. He mimed picking her up and pointed to the fire. "I must take her to where it's warm."

Without hesitation, he lifted her to his chest. He saw the severity of her condition and spoke to her in soothing whispers. "You, my mysterious one, may be beyond our ability, but not the mountain's."

He carried the girl closer to the common fire in the center of the village and laid her on a blanket. Yenene examined the girl while a clay pot of fresh water boiled over the fire. Her clothes looked unlike anything he had ever seen. The feathers were knitted and secured in a fashion unlike the villagers' weaving, and they graced her frame in a most elegant way.

Her bloodied and broken arm stained her white down and hung lifeless at her side. Her pale face looked stark white against the gray day. The medicine man pressed his ear to her heart; its beat was shallow and weak. He bound a leather strap to her broken arm above the protruding bone to stop the bleeding, then with the water from the pot, he washed her wounds and bruised face.

Kwanita approached and spoke softly to Yenene. "It

took great confidence for the mountain eagles to put her in our trust, but their girl is badly hurt. She has lost much blood—too much."

"Yes," he said, "her heart is growing weak and I fear for her life. Where is Bending Tree?"

"Our chief has gone with Pony and Honovi to look for the healing-stone taken by the foreigners. They should have recovered it by now."

Yenene felt anxious. "I must go and find them. There may yet be hope for her before night falls."

Yenene studied the face of the girl again and stroked her tangled hair. His thoughts went back to a time when a man with hair like hers fell from the sky. A healing-stone saved the man and the chief back then; surely it would help her now, if it weren't too late.

"I'll go at once." He jumped to his feet and ran to where the horses were tethered, calling two men to him. "Takota, Tamarack, come with me."

High on the mountain, in a garden of towering rocks, a large boulder moved. It twisted and turned until it uprooted, then it slowly toppled with an echoing thud. Dust stirred the air. The stone scooted forward through the haze and stopped. From the earth where the boulder had been, a warm, teal light glowed in pulsating beams.

Arms of rippled granite emerged from the hole and pulled the solemn face of Igneous above ground, followed by his rocky torso. The guardian rolled out of the freshly-dug hole and stopped next to where Windy's broken body rested. He hung his head and stroked her wing tenderly.

"Dear Windy." He could barely speak her name. He

scooped her into his arms and, holding her as lovingly as a father cradles his newborn, rocked her in one arm and stroked her head with the other. He cringed when he saw her chipped beak and a sizable patch of feathers missing from neck to shoulder. Tears rushed down his stricken face and evaporated with a hiss when they hit the ground.

The strong arms, that moments before had moved earth and stone, now trembled under a bouquet of bloody feathers. "Peace be with you a little too soon, my young one. Much sooner than the earth will see peace, I'm afraid. You shall not be forgotten, my Windy of the Mountain," he choked-up through the words. "Your death shall not be in vain, I promise."

Without taking his eyes from her, he turned and laid her body on a rock, then he scooted backwards, keeping strict watch over her until he reached the opening of the tunnel.

He reflected on her life: her first awkward flight, her curiosity beyond the borders of Elysium, her daring visit into the mouth of Misty, her concern for the unfortunate, and her adoption of a baby girl. There would not be another like her.

After a time, he turned, reached inside the tunnel, and lifted out a crystal bowl filled with the purest water Misty could find. In the midst of the bowl rested a single living-stone as bright and beautiful as any gem that ever sparkled in the sun. Igneous went back to Windy and set the bowl beside her. Taking her once more in his arms, he washed her wounds and cleaned her feathers.

Not ready to acknowledge her death, he decided to think of her as only sleeping. As deep and ancient as time itself, he sang an old lullaby in a forgotten language, a song about all things new in a land of plenty:

"Sjaun do law la logra, Ta perl la jauk ow may
Pala do seeka hamma, ku kala pu sala mu nay
Hombra sjaun lue kika lue kika sjuan sjuan
Law law macka sue shena sue shena mazuan"

When Igneous finished preparing Windy, he positioned himself over the blood-stained soil and spun in circles, building up momentum. He ground himself against the rocks and hardened earth until he stood in a hole a good four feet deep and eight feet across. Then he took the glowing stone and placed it in the middle of the grave, where it pulsated with life, just as it had done since the birth of the planet.

He took Windy once more in his arms and rocked her gently. No more tears came, but his sorrow remained. He placed her over the stone within the hole and fixed her wings as if she were diving from the sky. Finally, he lifted his hand to his stony lips for a kiss and touched it to her scarred beak as a final goodbye.

Once out of the grave, he lifted his head to the sky, observing the birds frolicking in play as if nothing serious had or would ever happen. The small pikas barked out to each other from the rocks around the mountainside. Sprigs of wildflowers reached for sunlight around the monstrous boulders, searching for their solar food. Creation remained as it should be, he thought, carefree and living for the day. Not so for him, at least not this day.

Igneous' thoughts turned to a different matter. He pondered the massive boulder he'd uprooted and ran his skilled hands over its face, examining it with the eye of a sculptor. He placed his hand in a calculated position, tore a chunk off and cast it aside. He repeated the action methodically, placing his hands in a certain spot and crumbling the stone as if it were dirt clods. Again and again he ripped at the boulder and the tillings grew higher. In a short time, he rolled the stone over to the other side and continued tearing until a recognizable form took shape.

Pleased at the rough draft, he took his finger and etched detailed lines. He turned the immense boulder, sculpting as he went.

The day wore on and still he continued etching the details. Finally, with the palm of his hand, he rubbed over the surface, sanding it smooth. He gazed over his creation and a glimmer of a smile crossed his face.

"Ah, perfect, my child, perfect. One more thing and all will be ready; you'll see."

Igneous rolled to the foot of his sculpture. With his finger, he diligently carved three beautifully-scribed words on the underside of the base. He blew away the dust and stood back pondering the three words as if remembering something wonderful from long ago.

Satisfied with what he'd written, he pushed the wide base of the statue to the tomb's edge and, with a single thrust, he erected the monument so that it covered Windy's grave completely.

A storm of emotions passed over his face as he regarded the monument. There, amidst the boulders of the mountain, the vast figure of an eagle stood in silent testimony with its head thrust up and its wings arched down to the ground. Threatening, yet elegant to behold, it looked out like a sentinel across the tumbled slopes, the forest, and the distant hills. Its details were flawless in every way—an exact replica of Windy.

Igneous laid both hands on the monument and hung his head in silent prayer, paying his last respects. One more tear managed to squeeze past his lids. With all things properly said and done, he disappeared back into the hole from which he'd come, packing dirt and rocks behind him like a pocket gopher.

Chapter 21
The Human Touch

Blood flowed weak through collapsing veins and arteries; the heart begged for more fluid so it could do what it was created for, but found little for the job. The body's cells and vital organs starved for oxygen—death loomed imminent. The heart beat slower until the pulse was of no use; the body fell to the point of no return. Death reached for its prize.

Suddenly, like lightning flashing in a dark cave, the body exploded with life. It started with the tongue, then flowed down to the stomach, swelling life in an avalanche rush so strong that the cold hand of death jerked back as if singed by fire. A tidal wave of power gushed from the heart, and sent wave upon wave of freshly-created blood barreling down hollow veins like a runaway toboggan through an icy tunnel. Organs recharged with new life. Cells restored to perfection and the skin radiated a glow rivaling a newborn's.

Mariah's eyes snapped open. With a jerk, she sat up gasping for breath.

"Oh! Dear Misty, she's awake!" Kwanita drew back,

spilling a little of the stone's lifeblood down Mariah's chin.

The night's edge nibbled at the evening by the time Yenene finally returned with the chief and the healing stone.

Bending Tree knelt next to the girl, holding the other half of the stone—its contents dripping from his fingers. "So I see," he said, observing the vibrant teen. "It looks as though the stone reached her in time after all."

Shadows from the evening fire flickered across their faces. Bending Tree sighed in relief and put the half-shell aside. He leaned forward, looking into the blue eyes of their guest, and a grin wrinkled his face. "You are safe, daughter of the mountain." He placed a warm, soft hand over hers with a light squeeze.

Mariah had no recollection of human contact. The touch was like water to the thirsty—an incredible comfort she drank in—a comfort the eagles could never duplicate.

A few eagles, seeing her awake, floated in from the surrounding trees, but the fire kept them from venturing in all the way—except for Screaming Eagle, who trotted in anyway with a look of relief.

Mariah jumped to her feet. She had no idea where she was or how she'd gotten there. Instinctively, she ran to her grandfather's side, lifted his wing and hid underneath.

"Mariah." Her grandfather poked his head under his wing. "It's okay, child, come on out."

"Where are we?" she whispered.

"The man village, they're—"

Author:

Guy Brooke grew up fascinated with the lyrical words of songs and wondered if he, too, could evoke such emotions? Years later, he has written more than one-hundred songs, produced two self-published music albums, crafted and directed four original musical plays, and conducted five guitar concerts through San Juan College in Farmington, New Mexico. Writing rhyming stories for children and young adult fantasy novels proved to be a natural crossover for him.

Guy loves life, loves the young, and loves to write. Residing in Naches, Washington with his wife, Barbara, he wishes to continue manipulating words for the young readers until carpal tunnel takes its toll :)

www.guybrooke.com

Illustrator:

As a well-rounded artist; Arielle Chandonnet primarily focuses on representational painting, portraiture and visual problem solving. She is trained and has experience with most traditional media, as well as Adobe Photoshop and 3D modeling. She aspires to succeed as an independent artist and continues to build her personal portfolio and pursue freelance projects such as the illustrations for Mystical Mountain Magic which she created using Photoshop.

You can view all of Arielle's work at:

www.ArielleChandonnet.com